"Are you sure that it's okay if I stay, Kevin?

"I can go. I'm sure that I can stay with—" She stopped before she said Brittany. Her only other friend didn't have a place in her life for Heather's mess. She had her hands full dealing with the fire at her house. "I can stay at a hotel or something."

"You're not staying at a hotel." Kevin set her bag next to the wall, but his movements were awkward and tight. "You're welcome to stay here as long as you need."

"Kevin, I... Thank you." She didn't know what to say. *Thank you* just didn't seem like enough when what she really wanted to say was that he was part of the reason she had the strength to leave.

He had shown her there could be more in the world. That there could be something besides heartbreak and the constant thoughts that she could be doing something more to make someone else happy, even if that meant being miserable in her own skin.

Kevin had saved her life and he probably didn't even realize it.

SMOKE AND ASHES

—

DANICA WINTERS

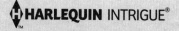

This book is dedicated to those men and women who have lived through the
turbulent cycles of abuse. May this book help you find your voice,
live your truth and experience the love you desire.

This book would not have been possible without the support from a multitude
of firefighters and law enforcement agents, including: Sergeant Ryan Prather,
Retired Training Officer Jerome Kahler, and the men and women of the
Frenchtown Rural Fire Department. Thank you for taking the time to help answer
questions and making sure that events portrayed in this novel were accurate.
You make this world a safer place.

A thank-you cannot be complete without thanking Lane Heymont, Denise Zaza
and the Harlequin team. Thank you for helping to bring this book to life.

ISBN-13: 978-0-373-69907-0

Smoke and Ashes

Copyright © 2016 by Danica Winters

Recycling programs
for this product may
not exist in your area.

Printed in U.S.A.

Danica Winters is a bestselling author who has won multiple awards for writing books that grip readers with their ability to drive emotion through suspense and occasionally a touch of magic. When she's not working, she can be found in the wilds of Montana testing her patience while she tries to hone her skills at various crafts (quilting, pottery and painting are not her areas of expertise). She always believes the cup is neither half-full nor half-empty, but it better be filled with wine. Visit her website at danicawinters.net.

Books by Danica Winters

Harlequin Intrigue

Smoke and Ashes

CAST OF CHARACTERS

Kevin Jensen—Fire inspector for the city of Missoula, Montana, and devoted father of two children struggling to find a balance between his family and the need to investigate a string of potentially deadly arsons.

Heather Sampson—Homemaker who dreamed of becoming a nurse, but now that her life is falling apart, she is attempting to find who and what she truly values in life.

David Sampson—Egocentric cardiologist and Heather Sampson's estranged husband. Prone to being volatile.

Brittany Miller—Heather's best friend, a homemaker and often the life of the party.

Nathan Miller—Brittany's husband and David's coworker at the local hospital. Loving, jovial and often too trusting.

Lindsay Jensen—Kevin Jensen's nine-year-old daughter.

Colter Jensen—Kevin Jensen's teenage son. Loves baseball, and is having disciplinary problems in school.

Battalion Chief Steven Hiller—Missoula City firefighter who heads active scenes and fire crews.

Elke Goldstein—Waitress at a local diner and the first victim in a string of arsons.

Tracy Jones—Elke Goldstein's neighbor and witness to arson.

Jeremy Lawrence—Detective and friend to Kevin Jensen.

Prologue

He looked down at Heather Sampson as he pulled the matchbox from his pocket. The box dropped from his hand, spilling matches onto her bedroom floor in a heap of deadly promise. Crouching down, he scooped them back into the container, careful to move quietly, afraid that at any second she would awaken and find him standing over her.

Her eyes were closed and her lips slightly parted, as if she waited for a kiss from her Prince Charming. She should have known better. There was no such thing as Prince Charming. There were only toads and a precious few men like him—men who worked to make everything just.

The sad truth was that there was no justice in marriage—at least not in any of the marriages he had witnessed. No. Marriage was one lie after another. One hurt feeling masked with a fake smile, only to have another lie strip it away. It was an endless cycle of pain.

What was the point? What was it all for?

As far as he could tell, it was for nothing more than ego and some idealistic hope that if they acted happy, if they faked it well enough, maybe they could finally believe it themselves.

He was here to make her a martyr, not that she would understand, but this was his chance to show her and the world what her marriage truly was—nothing more than smoke and ashes. A fire that had yet to burn itself out. But at last the time had come. The hour was here for him to stoke the flames and let them consume every crumb of her failing marriage.

The inferno could have it all.

He walked out of her bedroom and made his way downstairs, where the glorious scent of gasoline filled the space. Unlike the others, Heather's house would go up in a flash. In one giant fireball the whole charade would be over—the secrets, the lies, the fake smiles and the hurt feelings. It would all be gone and all her pain could be for a higher purpose.

The night air blew into the house, diluting the gas's perfume. He made sure to leave the door open as he stepped out and walked toward the garage. A puddle of gas sat on the sidewalk, just waiting for him.

He struck the match.

It was so much easier this way.

The fire's smoke curled skyward, creating a trail that led to the heavens. If he had his way, life would be better and she would be free.

Chapter One

A few days earlier

The note had been simple. Two little words. Two haunting, terrifying and humbling words. Words that had the power to rip out Heather's heart.

I'm leaving.

The paper sat on the kitchen counter where David had left it, a glass of water as a paperweight. The condensation on the glass had dripped down, leaving a ring of water. Like her tears, it was long dried, but it would never disappear.

She fought the urge to turn around and leave the kitchen, lunch be damned for the second day in a row, but the pressures of the day and her nagging hunger drove her forward, past the stained note on their newly installed granite countertops to their perfectly polished stainless-steel fridge.

David had been adamant that they have the finest of everything—the finest appliances, the finest table, all the way down to the silk table runner they'd had specially made and shipped from India. Now, in the lifeless kitchen, the bloodred runner made the entire room seem like a picture out of a home decor magazine, but nothing like a home.

None of it had ever really mattered, not when all she was left with was an empty kitchen and anger in her gut.

Opening the fridge, she was met with its cold, stale air. The only contents were a single bottle of Perrier and a half-eaten piece of week-old cheesecake. God, she loved cheesecake. The way it melted on the tongue, leaving behind the luxurious texture of butter. David hated for her to have it, complaining it made her gain weight.

She grabbed the plate and folded back the plastic wrap. David could hate the cake and her all he wanted. He had made it clear he was *leaving*. If she wanted to eat cake, she could. He wasn't here to stop her.

Grabbing a fork, she stabbed the tines into the cake and lifted it to her mouth. The scent of cream cheese filled her senses, making her mouth water. David would have hated this defiance.

She threw the fork and the uneaten bite into the sink and dropped the cheesecake, plate and all, into the garbage bin. David would come back. He always came back. And when he did, he would know she had gone against his wishes.

She stared down at the garbage. David would notice the plate was missing from the stack of exactly eight.

She had every right to be angry, but she would pay if he thought she had done something to intentionally upset him.

Reaching into the bin, she retrieved the plate and scraped the cheesecake off the edge. She couldn't disappoint him no matter how much he disappointed her.

She stood at the sink and washed the plate as she

stared outside. There had been so much more that she had wanted to do with her life. When she'd been young she had dreamed of helping people, of being a nurse. She smiled as she thought of her old teddy, Mr. Bear, who'd always stood in for a tragic victim of some terrible accident. She would use Band-Aid after Band-Aid fixing his wounds. Now he sat at the top corner of her closet, a reminder of a path not taken.

Because of David, she had given up everything,

There was a knock on the door and she set the plate in the drying rack. Reality was calling. Grabbing David's note, she stuffed it into her pocket.

There was another knock, this time harder, more urgent.

"Coming." She made her way out to the living room.

Looking in through the window in the door was her neighbor Kevin. He smiled and his eyes lit up as he saw her. As he moved, his sexy, prematurely graying hair sparkled in the sunshine. Heather tried not to notice the wiggle of excitement she felt at seeing him.

She opened the door. "How's it going?"

"Great, but I need your help," Kevin said. "I just got called to work. Do you think you could keep Lindsay for a while?" He pushed his daughter out from behind his legs.

Lindsay clutched the straps of her pink backpack. "Hi, Mrs. Sampson."

"Hi, sweetheart. Why don't you come in?" Heather dropped her hand onto the girl's shoulder and gave it a reassuring squeeze. "I'm glad you're here. I got a bunch of new craft supplies. There's a new bracelet designing kit you'll love. And I needed a friend today."

"Awesome!" Lindsay beamed.

"Thank you so much, Heather. I don't know what I'd do without you." Kevin reached out. "Lindsay, can I get a hug before I go?"

Lindsay threw herself into her father's arms. Kevin closed his eyes and squeezed her as if no one was watching. "Love you, honey. Be good, okay?"

"Okay, Daddy." Lindsay let go.

"Don't forget you have a peanut butter and jelly sandwich in your backpack if you need a snack."

Lindsay nodded.

Kevin turned to leave and Heather couldn't help but glance down at his black uniform pants. As he moved, they seemed to hug the muscular shape of his body. Warmth rushed through her.

"Wait," she called out to him, hoping to see his handsome, slightly mischievous grin one more time. "Where's Colter?"

He looked back and the grin reappeared, making the heat in her core intensify. "He had baseball this afternoon. He should be done in time for the Millers' barbecue. You going?"

Weeks ago David had promised they would go, but now, with everything that had happened between them, he would never agree.

"I'm not sure." Heather forced a tight smile.

"I hope you do. It'd be nice to catch up." Kevin paused. "I'll be back to pick her up as soon as I can."

Heather nodded. "No rush." She needed all the excuses she could get to keep from having to focus on her life, and a nine-year-old girl and her much-too-handsome father were the perfect distractions.

"Thanks!" Kevin rushed off, heading toward his

white truck that was emblazoned with the golden words *Fire Inspector.*

Heather pasted a smile on her face as she closed the door. Everything would be okay. "You ready for some fun, Lindsay?"

"I need to do my homework. It's due tomorrow."

"Homework? You only have a few weeks of school left."

Lindsay shrugged as she sat down in her regular spot on the couch. She took out her worksheets. "It shouldn't take long."

"You need me to go over it with you?" Heather silently wished she could help.

"Nah, I got it. Thanks, though."

Her hope deflated. "Okay. I'll be in the kitchen. Let me know if you change your mind. When you're done we can make those bracelets."

"Okay," Lindsay said, sounding preoccupied.

Heather walked back into the lifeless kitchen, picked up her cell phone and unlocked the screen. She tapped in David's phone number and when the phone rang her stomach twisted with nerves. He would pick up, wouldn't he?

It rang again.

"Why are you calling?" he answered.

"No 'hello'?" Heather asked, trying to keep her anger from seeping into her voice. "I thought maybe by now—"

"By now what? That I'd want to come back to the house?" David growled. "Listen, Heather. We can't keep doing this. Did you get my note?"

Her fingers moved to the letter in her pocket. "I did, but I was hoping—"

"What?" he interrupted. "That I didn't mean it?"

"David, we can work this out. We just need to go to counseling. I would do it for you." She pulled the note from her pocket and flattened it on the island.

"If we went to counseling that would imply that there's something to save. At this point, Heather, just seeing you makes me sick."

Her knees gave out under the weight of his words and she fell onto a barstool. "I'm sorry, David. I didn't mean—"

"Sorry doesn't cut it, Heather. I told you that you weren't allowed to talk to Andrew anymore. I see the way you look at him. And the way he looks at you. You're having an affair." David paused. "Don't you care how it makes me look that you're sleeping with another doctor?"

When she'd seen Andrew at the Easter fundraiser for the American Heart Association, he'd been overly friendly—maybe even approaching flirtatious with her—but it had been nothing more than banter. If David hadn't kept bringing up the incident, she would have forgotten it by now, but David wouldn't let it go, no matter how much she pleaded.

"I'm not. I never—"

"If you're not having an affair, then why did I see you talking to him outside the hospital the other day?"

She stared at the wrinkles in his note. "He stopped me. He just wanted to ask about you. I told him you didn't want me to talk to him, but he wouldn't listen."

"Was he trying to find out the next time it was safe to come into our house and screw you?"

Hot, unwelcome tears rolled down her cheeks. "It was nothing like that. He just wanted to know if you're okay."

"What did you tell him?"

"Nothing. I didn't tell him anything."

"Do you think I'm stupid? That I don't know when someone's lying to me?"

"I promise. I never lied. Just come home," Heather said, her voice like that of a trapped animal. "Tonight's Brittany's barbecue. Please, you have to go…"

"First you have an affair, and now you want me to come home? You are nothing, Heather. Why would I want to be seen with a woman like you?"

She crumpled his note in her hand. She wasn't weak…but it was hard not to be crushed when the world around her was collapsing.

Chapter Two

The windows of the sage-green house were intact, and a basket full of half-dead pink flowers waved lazily in the breeze as Kevin parked his truck. Aside from the flurry of motion and yellow caution tape, it would have been hard to tell this had been the location of an active fire.

Something about the place reminded him of Heather. Maybe it was the way it seemed so perfect, so put together on the outside, but if he looked a little deeper he saw whispers of turmoil within. Yet, with the house, he could open its doors and uncover its secrets, whereas with Heather there were too many things standing in the way—he could never truly know her.

A fire crew milled around the yard as they mopped up the scene, and the battalion chief, Stephen Hiller, was writing something in his notepad. Kevin killed his engine and the BC turned and gave him an acknowledging tip of the head. Hiller's face was pinched and his eyes tired, as though he was just waiting for him to arrive so his crew could hand off the chain of custody.

On the porch of the neighboring white row house a little boy, his thumb in his mouth, sat in a turquoise patio chair. The boy smiled and waved at him, his chubby arm wiggling.

Something about how the boy's eyes lit up reminded Kevin of Colter when he'd been younger. Colter used to love waiting on the porch for him to come home. The second he'd arrived, his son would rush down the steps in a hurry to welcome him.

How things had changed.

For the millionth time, he wished he could turn back the clock, but life was fickle and moments fleeting. If he'd only known then what he knew now, he would have run to Colter and scooped him up in his arms and carried him inside to where baby Lindsay had been. He would have spent every spare moment he had with his wife and his perfect little family. Yet, most nights, he had just pat him on the head as he brushed past him on his way toward the fridge and a cold beer.

Allison had hated his routine, the way he was so wrapped up in his job when he'd come home from work. She had never understood how badly he'd needed a moment to wind down, to relax after a crazy day fighting fires. Then again, he had never really understood what it must have been like for her, waiting for someone to come home, only to have him arrive in body but not in mind.

There was no going back.

The little boy's mother opened the door and hustled the boy inside. After a moment the curtain in their living room shifted slightly as if the woman was watching.

Hiller walked up to the truck and tapped on the window. "Glad to see you could make it, Jensen."

"Sorry I'm late. I had to find someone to watch Lindsay." His thoughts moved back to Heather, the way her hair had haloed her face and her jeans had hugged her perfect hips when she'd answered the door.

Hiller nodded, but it was easy to see from the puckered look on his face that he didn't really understand—or care.

"We've been waiting an hour."

"I'm here now."

"Next time be quicker about it. Some of us have work to do."

"What, do you have a girlfriend waiting?" Kevin joked, but Hiller's face remained motionless. Kevin coughed, trying to dispel some of the tension. "Anyways… Ya wanna fill me in?"

"The crew arrived on scene at 5:03 a.m. I arrived a few minutes after. Fire started on the second floor. They managed to get the homeowner—one Elke Goldstein—out of the house in a matter of minutes."

"Anyone else in the house at the time of the fire?"

Hiller scanned his notes. "She was the only one. I asked her a few questions, but Ms. Goldstein wasn't especially forthcoming with information. She seemed relatively unharmed, but was adamant she had to leave."

"Do you know anything about her? Does she work? Is the house underwater?" There were no for-sale signs in the yard and the grass was well-kept, but it was amazing how good a house could look even when the owner was only a piece of paper away from losing it.

"As far as I know, everything was on the up-and-up, but she didn't really want to talk to me."

"Making friends again?"

"What the hell's that supposed to mean?"

"Just that you're popular."

"Why don't you stop worrying about me and start worrying more about your investigation?"

Kevin chuckled. "You know where Ms. Goldstein went?"

"She said she had to go to work. Someplace called Ruby's."

Kevin grabbed his clipboard. "What else can you tell me about the fire?"

"Fire was small. Confined to the second floor. Extinguished quickly. There was a suspicious mark in the upstairs hallway."

"Was anyone seen running from the scene? Anything suspicious?"

"One of her neighbors…" He pointed to the white house where the boy had been sucking his thumb. "They reported seeing a man leave the house a few minutes before the smoke started."

"Ms. Goldstein didn't tell you about him?"

Hiller shook his head. "Not a word." He handed Kevin a copy of the fire report. "Here're my notes. I've been more than thorough."

"Great." He clipped the report in his clipboard.

Hiller turned around to face his crew. "Let's go, guys. Now this is someone else's problem."

"Wait. Leave me a couple of guys. I need them stationed outside the door until I'm done."

"How long you want to keep the scene intact?"

Chief Larson's words echoed in his mind—*Things are tight, Jensen. We need to cut costs.* If he didn't watch it, he would be getting the ax. But he had to get back to Heather's to pick up Lindsay, and he had promised Colter he would swing by his baseball practice. Heather would help him, if he needed—she always did—but something in her beautiful, hazel eyes told him that today was one of those days that she needed him. He couldn't let down her or his kids.

"I'm going to need at least a day or two."

"Jensen, time costs money—money the city won't give us. What little we have would be better spent on something other than chasing down a ghost. You know the chance of finding whoever is behind this is slim to none. Don't waste my time and the taxpayer's money. Let the insurance company write her a check."

"I'm trying to save the taxpayer's money by stopping this from happening again."

"You haven't even been in the house yet, Jensen. Who the hell knows? Maybe it was just some kid playing around. Why do you always have to assume the worst?"

"Hoping for the best is a rookie mistake."

Hiller slammed his fist against the truck. "This is coming out of your budget."

"No problem," he lied.

The fire inspector's budget was closer than a hair on a gnat's ass every month. If he found adequate evidence of arson, maybe he could convince the chief to cover the cost of keeping the chain of custody going for the next thirty-six hours, but probably nothing more.

"You need to step into line with the rest of the department, Jensen," Hiller threatened. "It's been long enough since Allison died. You're starting to cost us money because of your inability to do your job."

He cringed. Why did Hiller have to remind him? The weeks and months after Allison's death, he'd get into the flames and all he'd been able to think about was his wife, sitting in her hospital bed as the chemo burned through her veins.

Three years ago, after Allison's death, the department had taken him out of the fire and put him in an office chair, but even as fire inspector things weren't going as they should be. He'd been taking too long on investigations, but he rationalized it by telling himself that he was holding his responsibilities to a higher standard than his predecessor—a senior firefighter who had been happy playing by the unwritten rules while he sat back and waited to collect his pension.

"I've got this, Hiller."

"Time is money, Jensen."

"Do I need to remind you of our motto: *protecting lives and saving property?* Lives come first, Hiller. Money isn't even in the equation."

Hiller glowered at him but said nothing.

"Just give me the men I need."

Hiller looked out at his crew. "The rookies can stay behind." He pointed at two twentysomethings that had just been hired. "You guys monitor the house!"

They nodded and walked to the front of the yard.

Hiller turned back to him. "Get this handled. I need my guys. Our work actually makes a difference." Then he stormed off.

Kevin ignored the retreating cavalry as he looked down at Hiller's notes. At least he had a description of the man—dark haired, around six feet tall and an average build.

His handset sat in the window, and he stared at it for a moment before deciding to leave it there. He wasn't a real firefighter; nothing he did was an emergency. As Hiller was more than happy to point out, his job rarely made a difference. He was little more than a glorified desk jockey, filling out paperwork and teaching kids about smoke detectors.

He stepped out of the truck and slipped into his bunker gear and boots, making sure to grab his investigation kit and helmet before he made his way toward the house.

There was less than an hour before Colter's practice was over. He had to make a pass through the scene and take some notes, but then he could get across town to the high school to catch the tail end. If he hurried, Colter wouldn't notice he'd been missing. Maybe he would even get a chance to talk to Heather and thank her for her help.

Perhaps he could convince her to come to the barbecue. She always looked beautiful at those things—her naturally tan skin finally exposed after a winter hidden away. Last year, she'd worn her dark hair down. It had looked so soft, so touchable, just like her lips.

Those lips. He'd love to make those lips his.

He laughed at himself. Those lips, just like the rest of her, could never be his.

The only thing he could ever be to her was a friend, and that was only if he hurried.

He made his way around the back of the house, taking pictures every few feet. The door to the garage was unlocked and, as he opened it, the smell of burnt chemicals swirled around him. Thick black residue coated everything, including the woman's car, but nothing was burned.

On the wooden steps that led to the house, there was a pair of discarded women's flip-flops and beside them was an oily black shoe print. The print had a star pattern at its center and rectangular squares around the sole's edges. He snapped a picture. It was probably a leftover of someone walking through the oil slick in the garage while they'd made their way inside. He took a swab of the substance and tagged it as evidence to be sent to the crime lab.

The whole downstairs dripped with water and his footsteps sounded like suction cups as he made his way through the kitchen. The small rectangular room was typical of a low-income home, linoleum on the floor, cheap oak cupboards and an apartment-sized refrigerator.

In the living room, there was black, sticky ash on the walls where the smoke had billowed through the house. A thick layer of oily soot covered every surface making it impossible for him to be able to lift fingerprints.

He followed the smoke pattern up the stairs, and the acrid smell grew stronger. In the center of the hallway, between two bedrooms and in front of the burned-out bathroom, was a black circular pattern.

Another V-shaped pattern started at the floor, and at its center was an electrical outlet. He looked up. The light had melted and it pointed like a finger to the blackened circle.

There was no doubt about it, he'd found his ignition point.

He crouched and wafted the air toward him as he took in a long breath of the oily, dirty smoke. It had a faint chemical smell.

Around the edges of the charred circle was a ring of white powder. He took another picture. Opening his bag, he pulled out an evidence can and scooped some of the white residue into it.

This fire was no accident.

An event like this, one started with chemical oxidizers, wasn't the work of a novice. This was someone who knew the chemicals required to start a fire. Plus they likely knew most chemical reactions took several minutes to ignite—giving them enough time to flee the scene.

If he had to bet, this was a person who would do it again.

According to the notes, Elke had been in her bedroom at the time of the fire. If the perp had wanted to kill her, they would have built a fire that she couldn't escape, yet they had kept it small, manageable.

He turned to his clipboard and wrote: *Suspect may not have meant to kill victim.*

He glanced down at his watch. Fifteen minutes before the end of practice. He was never going to make it to the baseball field in time to see Colter.

He put away his clipboard, labeled the evidence and dropped it into his kit.

The burden his job put on him was fine, but bit by bit and day by day, he could see Colter pulling away. It was even evident in the way his son walked, no longer the fumbling steps of a boy, but the saunter of a young man. Every time Kevin had a call lately, he had watched as Colter used this newfound gait to walk as far away as possible. After today and his broken promise, it would only get worse.

Chapter Three

David stomped into the house and slammed the door, the sound making Heather jump. The sweat on her palms made her hands stick to the edges of the kitchen counter, and they peeled off with a wet sound as she stood up to greet him.

His dark hair was perfectly shaped and his eyes bright, as if he hadn't had the same trouble she had sleeping last night. The only thing that gave away his anger was the slight tic of his lip, as though he was holding back a snarl.

"Hi, David," she said, trying to sound cool and indifferent but failing as fear and desperation crept into her voice.

"Don't talk to me. Don't think I came home for you."

"Are you going to come to the barbecue with me?"

"We'll both be there. I would hardly say we're going together."

Heather glanced over her shoulder toward Lindsay, who was sitting on the couch weaving thread around her bracelet.

"You look like crap," David said as he walked to the fridge and grabbed the unopened bottle of Perrier.

She closed the door to the kitchen. Lindsay didn't

need to hear anything David had to say right now. She would get the wrong idea. David wasn't a bad man, just stressed. Stress always brought out the worst in people.

"I should've known you would go to seed without me around." He smirked as he looked at her. "I don't know what you're going to do without me."

His words were like a fist slamming into her gut, but she tried to ignore the pain. She needed to fix this and get him back. She couldn't let herself fall into the same cycle her mother had—a life built around a husband who only came home when it was convenient and who was more than happy to use her love as a tool to manipulate her. She was better than that.

For a moment her mind moved to Kevin—he had never treated Allison the way David treated her. Yet that was in public. Who knows what happened behind closed doors. Perhaps all marriages were the same—one person always bending to the whims of another for the sake of commitment.

"I don't understand this, David. I don't even know where this is coming from."

"Do I have to remind you about Andrew?"

Heather flicked a glance over her shoulder. "Don't. Lindsay's here."

"You afraid she's going to find out what you've done?"

"I didn't do anything." The second the words fell from her lips, she wished she hadn't spoken back. Her insolence would only make things worse, and she needed him back—she needed to hold her family together.

David glowered. "I don't care what you say anymore. You're a liar and a cheat." He slammed the bottle on the granite countertop so hard Heather couldn't believe the emerald-green glass hadn't broken.

She slumped onto the stool as tears welled in her eyes.

David pushed back from her in disgust. "Save the waterworks for someone who gives a damn." He strode out of the room. "Lindsay, when you grow up don't be like her," he said as his heavy, angry footfalls thundered through the living room.

Heather moved to follow him, but stopped in the doorway. Lindsay glanced over at her but looked away when she met her gaze.

Heather wiped away her tears. "Don't worry, Lindsay." She tried to smile, but the simple action pained her. "David's just upset."

Lindsay just nodded.

"Really." The lie made her voice quake. "Everything will be okay."

"Okay, Mrs. Sampson." It was clear from Lindsay's averted eyes that there was no way to make her feel better or forget what had happened.

"Can you do me a favor, Lindsay?"

She finally looked up. "What?"

"I don't know what you heard, but can you please not tell your dad anything? I don't need him to…" She paused. He had so many things in his life that needed his attention. She couldn't let him sacrifice his time by helping her to deal with the storm in her personal life. No doubt, this storm would pass, just like the others that had preceded it.

"You don't need him to what?"

"I don't want him to worry."

Lindsay shrugged. "Okay, Mrs. Sampson."

The pipes clanked as David turned on the shower in the master bathroom.

"How's the bracelet coming along?"

"Fine." Lindsay lifted it for her to see. "You know, if you wanted, you could come with me and Dad to the Millers'."

Heather's smile came a little easier. "That's really nice of you, but you don't need to worry. I'll have to go up and talk to David, but I would guess that we're probably going together. Fighting is just what married people do."

KEVIN MADE HIS way toward Heather's house where Lindsay waited. David's Porsche was in the driveway. Hopefully everything was going okay. Every time he was around, David treated him like the village idiot, and he always wrapped his arm around Heather as if she was some high school conquest rather than his wife.

He had always hated men like that.

There was no reason for two people in a healthy relationship to hover and mistrust one another. When Allison had been alive, he'd never needed to claim her. No. Anytime they had been together it was like they were magnetic. It hadn't mattered whether they were alone or in a room filled with people, he only saw her.

They had *fit*.

It was dumb luck he had found such a once-in-a-lifetime love.

Maybe it was stupid of him to compare what he and Allison had to anyone else. Maybe they hadn't had just a simple once-in-a-lifetime love. Maybe they were soul mates, their love created by the gods.

Either way, he appreciated Allison way more than David seemed to appreciate the special woman he had found in Heather. His neighbor didn't deserve such a woman—a woman so beautiful that the first time Kevin had met her she'd taken his breath away, a woman who put up with David's possessiveness, a woman who accepted the hours that a cardiologist worked. Who knew what else she was forced to accept. Bottom line— Heather deserved better. Whether she knew it was another thing.

Regardless, it was none of his business. And he shouldn't be thinking of his neighbor and his daughter's babysitter this way. Though, truthfully, she'd been in his thoughts way too often lately.

He parked the truck and walked toward the house. Every bush along the walkway was perfectly shaped into a little sphere—it was like a trail of bombs just waiting to explode.

He knocked on the door.

It creaked open. Heather's long brunette hair was pulled half up, making her look like one of those models from the Victoria's Secret catalogs that he kept hidden in his bedroom like a teenager. Quickly he envisioned her in the skimpy lingerie and his gaze drifted to her breasts, but he wrestled his attention away. He hardened at the thought of her undressed.

What was wrong with him today? There were so many other things he needed to be worried about besides how a friend looked naked.

"Hey. I'm glad you're here." She smiled, but it didn't reach her eyes. Something was wrong.

"Lindsay good?"

Heather's face tightened.

At the sound of his voice, Lindsay poked her head around the corner and smiled. "I gotta grab my backpack."

He turned back to Heather and looked into the darkness that seemed to fill her hazel eyes. "Are you okay?"

"I'm fine. Really. Just tired," she said, maybe a little too insistently.

"I appreciate your taking Lindsay, but if you have other things that you need to take care of, I can find something else to do with her. Colter's sixteen—he could be helping."

Heather leaned in close. "No teenage boy wants to babysit his sister. I'm sure he has other things on his mind." Her breath brushed his cheek. He breathed in, trying to control his body, but she smelled like flowers and the scent only made him harder.

"Yeah. Other things on his mind," he said, stumbling through his words. He tried to take that advice and thought about baseball and who won the 1996 American League pennant.

"Are you okay, Kevin?" Heather frowned.

"Yankees," he blurted out, trying to look anywhere but at her.

"What?"

"Nothing." He leaned in, through the open door, brushing lightly against Heather and her not-to-be-noticed-by-him breasts. "Lindsay, let's go!"

"Coming!" Lindsay said in a sing-song voice.

David came down the stairs and stopped beside Heather, barely giving her a sideways glance. He smiled. His teeth were straight with long, oversize canines. "Hi, Kev, how's it going?" He slapped him on the back. "Heading to the Millers' tonight? It's going to be a good one."

"Thought I'd pop in. Probably won't stay too long." The lust he had been feeling disappeared as he stared at David's predatory smile.

"Long day?" David wrapped his arm around Heather, but she seemed to freeze under his touch.

"Brutal."

When Lindsay made her way to the door, David turned and gave her a warm smile. "Thanks for coming by, hon. Great to have you here keeping the old ball and chain happy."

Lindsay stared at David, a confused look on her face. "Sure, Dr. Sampson." She slid past David, giving him plenty of space. "Bye, Mrs. Sampson. See you soon." She rushed to the car.

From Lindsay's befuddled look, he couldn't help wondering what he had missed.

He turned to Heather. "Everything go okay?"

"Of course. Always." Heather looked to David as though she was checking to make sure she was saying the right thing.

"We have a few things to discuss." David pushed Heather back and moved to close the door. "Talk to you later, Kev."

"It's Kevin."

David didn't seem to notice; instead, he turned toward Heather. As the door closed, Kevin could swear his face was contorted with rage.

Chapter Four

The teak chair pinched Heather's leg as she perched on the edge trying to make her legs look sexy. David wasn't even looking at her; instead he stood chatting away with Heather's beautiful friend Brittany. He brushed back Brittany's blond hair and whispered something. Her laughter cut through the air.

The grill sizzled and smoke poured into Heather's face, making her look away. A group of teenage boys were splashing around in the pool as the teenage girls sat on the side whispering behind their hands and texting on their bubblegum-pink phones.

Life had been so much simpler at that age. Days consumed with flirting and laughter. Nights filled with dreams of things to come. When she was close to that age she had been consumed with thoughts of the charming, too handsome, college-aged David—the man who had started their relationship with flowers and love notes and now couldn't even look her in the eye.

She walked over to him, but only Brittany looked at her. "Hiya, Heather. David was just telling me about his day. He's so funny!"

He hadn't been funny with her in a long time.

She suffered through a smile. "Yeah."

Brittany turned to David and laid her hand on his shoulder. "Did you tell her what happened?"

David finally bothered to look at her, but his eyes were pinched into a glare. "She doesn't like to hear about my job."

"What? Really?" Brittany giggled, the sound mimicking the titters coming from the poolside. "I think it's fascinating." She ran her finger down David's arm. "You have such a noble job—saving lives."

Heather couldn't stand the way David's face transitioned from a glare to a smile as Brittany touched him.

"I need a drink," Heather said.

Everything would be okay. She just needed to fake it and get through this day without breaking down and having everyone find out about her failing marriage.

"I'll go with you. Nathan's made the best strawberry margaritas." She looped her arm through Heather's and made her way toward the tiki bar.

Heather glanced back at her husband, but he'd already started to talk to another woman. Across from her, poolside, was Kevin. He sent her a sexy smile as he waved.

"Two margaritas, *por favor*!" Brittany called to her husband.

The winter-pale Nathan had on a coconut bra T-shirt, red hibiscus-covered Bermuda shorts and a party store straw hat. "Coming right up."

He shook his chest, making the coconuts jump. "Where's the smile, Heath?"

"I...uh..."

"She just hasn't had a drink yet. That'll make everything better. Isn't that right, bestie?" Brittany giggled and pushed her into a seat.

"Lime in the Coconut" came on the speakers and Nathan did his best impression of a hula dancer as he flipped on the blender. But not even the goofy Nathan could make her laugh today.

He poured the mix into a bowl-sized glass. As he sat the glass in front of her, the scent of tequila was strong in the air.

"Little heavy-handed with the tequila, huh?"

Nathan laughed. "I just want you to get to feeling better. Remember, it'll be better tomorrow."

She doubted it.

One of her neighbors, the woman from three doors down who always walked her Pomeranian in the mornings, stepped to the bar and drew Nathan's attention.

"So what's going on?" Brittany asked.

"Huh?" Heather took a long sip from the delicious, strawberry drink.

"You've barely spoken to David all day."

Brittany thought that his avoidance was *her* fault? Brittany was her best friend, but if Heather told her what was truly going on and how close she was to divorce, the gossip would fly faster than cottonwood fluff in spring. Then again, if she didn't explain, Brittany was likely to assume something far worse than the truth.

"We're going through a rough patch."

"I got that. I don't think I've ever seen you look at David like that before."

"Like what?"

Brittany chewed on her lip. "Well… You looked *desperate*." She said the word as if it left a foul taste.

She could hardly admit that she was desperate, or

Brittany wouldn't just carry the foul taste for the word, she would have a foul taste for her, as well. She couldn't lose her only girlfriend.

"It's hard, Brittany. One minute I can't imagine my life without him, and the next I'm so angry. I'm so confused."

"What do you want?"

"I don't know, but I can't give up." She may not love him at the moment, but her mother had always told her that love varied in marriage—now was just a low.

Heather took a drink, letting the tequila soak into her tongue. "How can I get him back?"

"You're talking to the right woman." Brittany wiggled her finger. "I've got just the thing."

"HAVE YOU SEEN COLTER?" Kevin asked, handing Lindsay a juice box.

She shaded her eyes as she looked up at him from beside the pool.

"Uh-uh. You think he's still at practice?"

Kevin glanced down at his watch. "He should've been done an hour ago."

"He's gonna come. It's okay, Daddy."

He nodded as he took out his cell and called his son. It went straight to voice mail.

"Colter, this is Dad. Sorry I missed your practice. I had a thing with work. Lindsay and I are at the barbecue. Where are you? Give me a call. Love ya, bud."

He slid the phone into his pocket and walked toward a long table filled with food. He popped a stuffed mushroom into his mouth, savoring the flavor as Bob Marley & the Wailers sang in the background.

His phone buzzed. "Colter?" he asked without looking at the screen.

"No, Kevin. It's Detective Lawrence. I got your message."

"Thanks for getting back to me. Did you get a chance to run by the house?"

"Yeah, your guys showed me around. Thanks for waiting."

"Sorry. I had a meeting."

"A meeting where they play Bob Marley?" Lawrence sounded annoyed.

"You know how it is," Kevin answered with an awkward laugh. He didn't need Lawrence to think of him as anything less than professional, and he was already on his last leg after leaving in the middle of an investigation. "Did you get a chance to pull up Goldstein's record?"

"She has a few citations, but nothing major. Certainly nothing that would make me think she would be behind an arson. Then again, it's the ones you don't see coming…" Detective Lawrence sighed. "You got any suspects?"

"I'm looking into it."

"You haven't spoken to Goldstein yet?"

"Not yet."

Kevin's breath caught in his throat as Heather made her way out of the back door of the Millers' house with Brittany close at her heels. He couldn't help notice she'd changed clothes. A pink miniskirt now hugged the round arch of Heather's hips and she wore a white shirt with a cut so deep that it exposed her navel. For a moment, everything and everyone at the block party went silent. The only sound was the lapping of the pool.

Lawrence said something, but Kevin couldn't make out his words.

She was so beautiful standing there with curves he never knew she had. The wind fingered the edge of the V-neck top, exposing the roundness of each of her breasts.

What would it be like to kiss that skin—that gorgeous, fresh skin? His mouth watered as he imagined running his lips over her body.

"Kevin, you there?"

"Huh?"

He tried to look away.

"Are you listening?"

"Sorry, what did you say?"

"I *said* let me know if you need anything."

"Sounds great. I gotta run," Kevin said, forcing himself to stop staring.

The woman was his neighbor. She was married. No matter how badly he wanted her, she was off-limits.

Chapter Five

Her mind swam in the relaxing surf of her second margarita. The world around her had mellowed; there were no more harsh whispers or judging stares. Just a hot pink miniskirt and Brittany by her side.

"You *have* this," Brittany whispered.

"You think he cares?"

Brittany rolled her eyes. "David's going to eat this up. You look beautiful."

Heather reached down and tried to inch the skirt lower. David always gawked at the women who wore this type of thing. Hopefully he'd be just as happy to see her in such an outfit.

"Here he comes." Brittany nodded toward David, who was staring wide-eyed at her. "I told you this would get his attention. From the looks of things, you got everyone else's, as well. I wish I got that kind of reaction." She giggled and gave Heather a quick side hug and then walked away. David strode over.

"What in the hell, Heather?" he seethed through a smile of gritted teeth. He grabbed her by the back of the arm and moved her so their faces were concealed.

She looked back over her shoulder. Every adult was

staring at them—even Kevin. His mouth was open, as if he wanted to say something, but she quickly looked away.

"Don't I look nice?" she said loudly, hoping David would catch the hint that they were on display.

"You look great," he said, but the way his fingers dug into her soft flesh said exactly the opposite.

He turned and nodded toward Nathan. "Thanks for dinner. We have to be going."

Nathan nodded and waved with a paper umbrella in his hand.

"What in the hell do you think you're wearing?" David dragged her out of the gate and toward his Porsche.

"You're hurting me. Please, let go," she said, her drink-slowed words coming out of her lips as though they were coming from someone else, someone bolder.

"I'm hurting you? Do you know how much you just embarrassed me?"

He'd been embarrassing her for years—when he hadn't shown up to dinner dates, when he had forgotten to come home at night and when he had called her names in front of their friends. Now he was telling her she was embarrassing him?

It might have been the margaritas, but she couldn't even look at him.

He pushed her into the passenger seat of his coupe and then went to his side and got in.

"You're such a slut."

A feeling of sickness rose in her throat.

"I'm not a slut," she said under her breath.

"What was that?"

"Nothing." She swallowed back the urge to vomit.

"Did you think Andrew would be there? Were you

parading yourself for him?" He looked her up and down. "He can do better."

"I don't know how to prove to you that I've never cheated."

The road buzzed by. "So you're a liar and a whore? Real classy. I married you to be a pure wife and a wholesome mother. First you couldn't give me the children I wanted, and now you're a cheater. There's no reason to keep you in my life."

"I…" She tried to swallow the sickness back, but it was no use. She threw her hands over her mouth. She tried to tell him to pull over, but it was too late. She was sick all over his black dashboard.

He'd never forgive her. He loved the car more than anything, and definitely more than her.

"What the hell!" He pulled the car to the side of the road. He reached across her and opened the door. "Get out! I'm never going to be able to get your stench out of the leather."

They were only a few houses away from theirs, but distance didn't matter… She was sick. If he'd been sick, she would have spent the rest of the day being the dutiful wife her mother had taught her to be. Yet he cared so little, he was kicking her out on the side of the road.

"I can't believe you, David."

"Get. Out." His fingers tightened on the steering wheel.

She grabbed her purse and stepped out of the car. He slammed the door and sped away with a spray of gravel.

Once again, she was alone, just as she had been as a child when her parents had fought. Sometimes it frightened her how much David reminded her of her father. They were cut from the same cloth, constantly berating and putting down their wives—and this time, instead of her mother, it was Heather being demeaned.

David stopped at their house. He didn't pull the car into the garage; instead he got out and walked in through the front door.

What would happen if she didn't go home?

David would probably love it. He'd never have to see her again. He'd get everything. All he'd need was a new wife. A wife to give him the family he'd always wanted—something he was only too happy to remind her she'd failed to give him no matter how hard she'd tried.

She stepped up onto the sidewalk and made her way toward the house. Before she could go inside she needed to clean herself up. She walked around the side of the house and washed up with the hose.

When she entered the kitchen, David threw a manila envelope at her.

"I've had the divorce papers written up. All you have to do is sign them. Do it now."

She stared at the envelope that lay on the counter just where his note had been only hours before. She didn't dare touch the paper out of fear that, if she did, it would make everything real.

"David…no…"

"Just sign the papers. You have to be as unhappy as I am."

For the first time in memory, she agreed with him. She wasn't happy. In fact, she couldn't remember the last time she had been happy with him. But that was what marriage was, right? It had ups and downs, and the job of both people was to make it work. Wasn't it?

"Things will get better. We just need to work together. Maybe you could take some time off. I don't remember when we spent real time together."

"Did it ever occur to you that I was avoiding you? We should've put a stop to this relationship a long time ago, but I know you're nothing without me. It was an act of sheer kindness that I've allowed you to be my wife this long."

Something inside her broke.

"You've *allowed me* to be your wife? Hasn't it occurred to you all I've given up to be with you? I gave up my education for you. I gave up my hopes of a job."

"A job," he said with a smirk. "That would take dedication."

"Just because you don't see it doesn't mean that I'm not dedicated—if I love something, I give it everything… Even if my love turns out to be misplaced." She looked at him and tried to control the hatred that welled within her.

"If you loved me so much, maybe you should have tried a little harder." He reached into a drawer and pulled out a pen and laid it on the envelope. "Just sign the paperwork. It's over."

She stared at the envelope but didn't move. "We made a promise to each other. You told me you never wanted to get a divorce. That marriage meant something to you."

"Marriage does mean something to me, Heather. It means fidelity, trust, honesty. You haven't given me any of those things."

She shook her head, trying to get rid of the ringing of his words. "Why do you always accuse me of something I haven't done? I've never given you reason to think—" She paused as a terrible thought came to mind. "Are you cheating on me, David? Is that what all this is about? Are you accusing me out of your own guilt? Are you trying to make yourself feel better about something you've done?"

"How dare you accuse me. I spend my days saving people's lives. I'm a damn hero." He ripped open the envelope and pushed the papers in front of her. "Sign them."

Her hands shook. It wasn't that she hadn't imagined the possibility of him asking for a divorce; she had just never thought it would be today.

There was no coming back from this—not right now. He was too angry. There was only one thing to do that could make it any better—she had to hold him off.

"I'll have a lawyer take a look."

"Don't you trust me, Heather?"

"If you had asked me two hours ago, I would've said yes. But now, it would be stupid if I did."

She picked up the papers and her car keys and walked out.

Chapter Six

After Heather's forced disappearance, Kevin hadn't been interested in the Millers' party and he'd found an excuse to leave. He shut his daughter's door. Surprisingly Lindsay had dropped into her bed without protest, just as she'd easily agreed with him to leave the party.

Colter sat behind his computer in his bedroom as Kevin made his way down the hall.

"Where were you, Colter?"

His son shrugged as he faced his screen. "I dunno."

"Try it again, bud. Where did you go after baseball practice?"

"Baseball practice ran long." He didn't turn around. "When I made it to the Millers', the party was over."

"You mind looking at me? I'm trying to talk to you."

His son shifted a few degrees in his seat. "What? I'm talking to you."

Kevin had never been much of a disciplinarian—that had always been more Allison's job. God, he wished she was here.

Once again he was reminded how badly he wanted a woman in their lives, someone he could share the ups and downs with, someone he could hold in his arms at night—someone like Heather.

"Is Heather going to come to my game?" Colter asked, as if he could somehow sense what was on Kevin's mind.

"I don't know. If you'd made it to the party, you could've asked her yourself. Where were you?"

"God, don't you get tired of asking the same questions? I told you… Baseball practice ran late. When I got to the party it was shut down. I didn't stick around."

"You don't expect me to believe that baseball practice lasted that long, do you?" Kevin leaned against Colter's door frame, half in and half out of the bedroom, just far enough in to let him know that he had his full attention, but far enough out that it wasn't a confrontation.

Then again, everything with Colter these days was a confrontation.

"Were you with a girl?"

Colter tapped at his keyboard. "No."

He was getting nowhere. "I would appreciate it if you would do as I ask. It's important that I can count on you, or else this free-for-all is going to come to a screeching halt. No more baseball. No more girls. No more friends."

His son spun around and cursed.

He twitched at the sound of his son's language. That was a new one.

"If you want to talk and act like a big man, that's fine, bud. But you need to know you're causing problems. I'm trying to do my best here. I'm sorry I can't be everywhere, but you aren't making this any easier. I need to trust you, okay?"

Colter's expression remained blank. He would make one hell of a poker player.

"Fine."

"Will you let me know when baseball practice runs late again? Please?"

"Fine."

"I love you, kid, but this attitude needs to come to an end." Kevin pushed off the door frame. "Get to bed. You have school in the morning."

Colter turned back around in his chair to face his computer. "Got it."

Kevin closed the door and walked into the living room.

Every day since Allison had died, some more of Colter seemed to fade. No matter how hard Kevin had tried, no matter how many parenting books he had read, he had failed at helping his son—just like he'd failed to save Allison. He couldn't help but feel as though he was on the brink of losing someone else he loved.

There was a knock at the door and he went to answer it, wondering who was calling on him now.

Heather stood on the top step. Her hair was disheveled, her eyes were red as if she'd been crying, her deep V-neck shirt was wet and soiled.

"What happened?" He motioned for her to come inside.

"I'm sorry. I didn't know where to go. Brittany wasn't answering."

"Come on in." He stepped aside. He would have asked her what was wrong, but after what he had seen at the barbecue there was no point.

She stumbled to the couch and sat with her feet curled beneath her. "Thank you." She dabbed at her eyes. "I hope I didn't wake you."

"No. I just put the kids to bed." He pointed at her shirt. "You want something clean to wear?"

She looked down and her mouth dropped open. "Oh, my God… Those damn margaritas."

"Be right back." He went to his bedroom and came back with a shirt. "Here, you can have this." He handed it to her and turned his back as she slipped off her V-neck. In the mirror by the door, he caught a glimpse of her naked breasts. He stiffened as he looked away. No matter how much he wanted to look at her, to take those puckered pink nipples into his mouth and make them his, she belonged to someone else.

"I'm done," she said. "Thanks for the shirt."

He turned but didn't know where to go, so he just stood there. "You're welcome."

Normally around women he was cool and collected. Yet with Heather, it was different. She was different. And no matter how badly he tried to break into work mode, treating her as though she was just another victim, he couldn't. He didn't feel right taking her by the hand and telling her it would all be okay. If he touched her, he might not be able to let her go.

"You want something to drink?" He moved toward the kitchen.

She stared into space. "David wants a divorce. He has the papers ready. I don't know what to do."

"What?" Kevin stopped and turned to her.

"Don't make me say it again. It doesn't feel real. None of this feels real."

"I get it." He felt like a moron, but he couldn't think of the right thing to say.

In a way, he'd been in her shoes when he had found out about Allison's death. A part of him had died in that moment. No matter how many times people said "I'm sorry," nothing could staunch the pain.

"I never thought this day would come. I mean…we've been unhappy. I thought maybe, but…I thought we'd make it through this. I should have seen this coming."

"When you love someone, sometimes you don't see what's staring back at you."

"What do you mean?"

He thought back to David hitting on Brittany at the barbecue. If Heather hadn't seen it, he was the last person who should tell her.

"Nothing. I just mean—"

"You think he doesn't love me?"

"I didn't say that," he said, mentally trying to back-pedal.

"It's okay. I know he doesn't. It's been a long time since…well, since I think he felt something other than contempt toward me. A divorce seems like the only answer."

"Is that what you want—a divorce?" The question came from a place inside him where he begged that she would say yes.

She didn't answer. Rather, she looked broken, as though she was a pane of glass that had been waiting for the strike of a hammer, and now that the blow had been struck, she'd come to him to help find the pieces.

He saved lives, but he'd never been good at rebuilding them—not even when the life was his own. He tried hard, but despite his efforts, Colter was a mess and he didn't spend nearly enough time with Lindsay. Everything he did was a struggle. Every choice was wrong or surrounded by guilt. He could never give Heather what she needed.

She wiped the tears from her eyes as she stood up and moved to him, her hips swaying with purpose.

What was she doing? She'd never looked at him like that before, with such intensity. If anything, she'd been overly insistent that they were friends...*good* friends, but that had been all. But that look, that light in her dark eyes, said there was something more—something he'd felt since the first moment he'd met her.

He must have been reading her wrong. He stepped back until he bumped into the table beside the door. "Heather..."

She put her finger on his lips, quieting him. Rising to her tiptoes, she swept her tear-dampened lips over the skin of his neck. Sparks of electricity shot down his body and reawakened a part of him that he had written off.

"What're you doing?" he tried to say, but it came out barely above a whisper thanks to the soft pressure of her finger against his lips.

She slipped his earlobe into her mouth and sucked. Oh, God... He wanted this. He wanted her.

He wanted to sweep her up in his arms and carry her to his bed. He wanted to wake up covered in her scent, to lick her flavor off his lips. Her kiss moved lower. Her tongue traced the neckline of his shirt. Her hands moved up his chest.

"Heather..." he moaned. "I want you..."

Before he could say another word, her lips met his. She tasted sweet, like warm berries right off the vine. How could a woman taste so good?

He wrapped his arms around her as he relished their kiss. He could do this forever...hold her forever...*be* with her forever.

The scent of sweetened alcohol wafted from her.

Kevin pulled back. Those lips, those pink, full lips weren't berry flavored—they tasted of margarita.

If she had been sober and come to him willingly and openly, it would have been hard for him to say no, but as it was, with her judgment skewed and muted by booze, there was only one choice.

"Heather…" He unwrapped his arms from around her body. "We can't do this. You can sleep here. You can have my bed. But tonight… *This* can't happen."

Chapter Seven

Heather rolled over in bed. Where her clock should have been was a glass of water and two red capsules she assumed were ibuprofen. The sides of the glass were beaded with sweat, reminding her of the letter that David had left behind.

The letter... The divorce papers... Oh...

She sat up but was forced back down by the *thump, thump, thump* of the bass drum beating in her skull. She picked up the pills and swallowed them down, anything to stop the pounding.

Light streamed through unfamiliar white curtains and she looked down at a dark gray shirt, underneath which was a miniskirt. She remembered Brittany's skirt but where had the T-shirt come from?

The bedsheets were yellow and soft, but those, too, were foreign.

She sat up more slowly, and this time the pounding of the bass drum changed to the *tom, tom, tom* of a timpani.

She pushed down the miniskirt and the simple action brought back a flash of her kissing Kevin, her hands sliding over the muscles of his stomach, her lips tasting the salty flavor of his skin.

Her body ached from what felt like gallons of tequila sloshing through her veins. At the very least she hadn't had sex with him—if she had, she could have never faced him again.

Hopefully he didn't think that her feelings were just some attempt at a drunken rebound. She had been foolish, but for her, it had sometimes felt as though there was more than a simple friendship between them.

She was such an idiot.

She tiptoed to the door and peered out into the empty hallway. This early in the morning everything was still. She slipped through the house and made her way outside, making sure to grab her shoes and purse by the front door.

The grass dripped with dew and not a single house's lights were on, with the exception of her and David's perfectly white house, where every single window was alight. He must have been awake all night, waiting for her.

Her stomach lurched, forcing her to run to the hedges that acted as a fence between the houses. She made it there in time to be sick.

There was a squeak of hinges as a door opened. She looked in the direction of the eerie, disquieting sound. David stood on their front step and glowered out at her.

His arms were crossed over his chest and his jaw was set, making him look like a dictatorial tyrant peering down upon his subjects.

"Get in the house."

She made her way to the door, carefully sidestepping him as she went inside. She could feel his glare upon her.

"Your catting around just saved me a lot of money."

Kevin tried not to think about Heather slipping away. He should have known that was exactly what she would do when she woke. Regardless, it still bothered him that she would run away as soon as she realized how badly he had wanted her.

Hopefully they could still be friends. Hell, maybe something more if her divorce went through, but something like that had to be months, maybe years, away from happening. For all he knew, last night had been her attempt at a one-night thing. Maybe she only wanted to get back at David. Maybe his was just the closest door.

Maybe, when it came to him, she didn't really care.

He wouldn't know how she felt until he saw her again. He didn't know whether to look forward to it.

Meanwhile he walked into Colter's room. He made his way through the mess and stopped at the side of his bed. Colter's chin showed the nicked signs of a recent battle with a razor. He reached up and pulled fuzz from a hair that had been missed. The hair was barely enough to be called a whisker, yet it was just another sign of the changes in their lives.

He leaned in and gave Colter a kiss on the head and drew in a breath, the way he used to when his son had been a baby. He no longer smelled of milk and baby powder, but rather he carried the odor of sweat with a pungent sock-scented kicker.

"Hey, bud," he said softly, trying to rouse him. "Time to get up."

Colter opened one eye and, seeing him, answered with a forgiving, sleepy smile.

There was still a chance to fix what was broken.

AFTER COLTER LEFT for school, Kevin dropped Lindsay off and made his way to the diner. No matter what was going on in his personal life, work awaited. At least in an investigation there was a chance he could get answers. It was black and white. Not like his mess of a private life.

His phone rang as he pulled the truck into a parking spot.

"Hello?"

"Inspector Jensen, this is Chief Larson."

"Hey, Chief, how's it going?" He tried to sound nonchalant.

"Not so great. I heard you and I may need to have a little meeting."

Kevin forced a laugh. "Come on now, Chief. I didn't do anything that bad, did I?"

"You were at last week's meeting, correct?"

"Yes, sir."

"Then you may have some idea why you and I would be having a problem."

"I'm aware that we're trying to cut back on costs. I understand and would love to comply with your request. However, sir, I must be able to do my job in a professional manner. *Protecting lives and saving property*— am I right, Chief?"

"Absolutely." There was a rustle as the chief moved the phone. "However, as I was made to understand, your investigation was impeded by your need to go to a neighborhood barbecue. Correct?"

His stomach clenched. How did Larson know?

"I did need to attend a social event with my family. It was an unavoidable situation." He tried his damnedest to make it sound like brain surgery instead of a party.

"So let me get this right, Jensen. You took two rookie firefighters and had them sit on an investigation that should have been buttoned up in one pass so that you could go to an *unavoidable social event*? Do you know how much you cost us? I had to call in two more firefighters and give them time and a half to cover for the ones you needed to retain your chain of custody."

"That wasn't my intention, sir."

"Your intention or not, this has to come to an end or I'm going to have to start cutting. We'd hate to lose you, Jensen."

"I'm working on the investigation now. I'll have this wrapped up soon." He walked up to the diner. Near the door was a newspaper kiosk where a picture of Elke's yellow-taped house blared out from the front page.

"I don't see why you need that much time."

"I've come to believe this may be the work of a serial arsonist. I'm hoping to pin down the suspect before there are any other fires."

"What makes you think it's a serial arsonist?"

"It's just my gut, sir."

"Your gut is going to cost me thousands…and possibly cost you your job. You need to get your butt over to that scene and pull the men off the lines."

He stared at the picture on the front page of the *Missoulian*. "I would, but I'd hate for the press to get the idea we aren't doing our best to keep the public safe. I mean it would look bad if there was another fire, a fire where someone was killed."

The phone rustled. "You've got thirty-six hours."

The line went dead.

He slid his phone into his pocket. The pressure was on.

Kevin walked inside and a sixtysomething waitress strode up to him.

"Can I help you, sonny?" she asked in the raspy voice of a lifelong smoker.

"I'm looking for an Elke Goldstein. She work here?"

The woman frowned. "Waddya want with her?"

"I'm just here to talk with her. I'll sit down and wait, if that's okay."

She grabbed a menu and led him to a table close to the kitchen door. "She'll be right out. Coffee?"

He mostly wanted answers, but coffee would do for now. "Sure. Thanks."

"Take it black?"

"Unless you can pour some of your sweetness in," he joked.

"Oh, we got a charmer, do we?" The woman strode into the kitchen with a wide smile on her lips.

A minute later a mousy, brunette woman walked out and stopped beside his table. She had a nice face, but her eyes told him she was a woman who worked long hours and dreamed of something more.

"I'm Elke." She scowled at him as she poured his coffee. "I know you?"

"The name's Kevin Jensen. I'm a fire inspector for the city of Missoula." He took a long drink of the ashy tasting coffee. "I was called to your house last night. Nice to meet you."

She took a step back from the table and looked over her shoulder. "How'd you find me? I thought y'all weren't going to bother me," she said, her voice tinged with a slight Southern drawl.

"Battalion Chief Hiller told me you worked here."

She nodded, but her body tensed and the pot in her

hand shook slightly, sloshing the coffee. "He had no business tellin' you. I didn't have nothin' to do with that fire."

In the fire academy, one lesson had been drilled into him over and over: It didn't matter what words came out of a person's mouth, body language and demeanor were a much better indicator of someone's guilt or innocence. Right now, Ms. Goldstein looked guilty. All he needed to figure out was whether she was guilty of setting the fire or guilty of something else.

"I'm sure you didn't have anything to do with it," he lied. "I just need to ask you a few questions so we can make sure you get the money you are entitled to from your insurance company." He paused as he let the bait sink in. "You do have insurance, don't you?"

"Yeah, I think so…" She looked away as though she was trying to catch a memory that had drifted out of reach.

If she had started the fire for the money, she would have known her house was insured, and for how much. But she wasn't innocent. She knew something.

"Miss?" A woman three tables down lifted her coffee cup.

Elke nodded. "I need to get runnin'. Want something to eat?"

He ordered the special, and as she turned to leave she said, "I get off in an hour. Meet me at the coffee shop 'round the corner. Sit in the back. Okay?"

"Got it."

"Good," Elke said.

SHE BARELY LOOKED at him while he sat and savored his breakfast, taking his time to dip his toast in his egg and drink three cups of coffee. Elke needed to feel the pressure. She needed to see that he wasn't going anywhere.

His phone buzzed.

"Hello, Mr. Jensen?" said a woman's nasal voice. "This is Ms. Farmer from Big Sky High School."

He stabbed his fork into his egg. "What did Colter do?"

"Colter hasn't arrived at school today. I was just calling to let you know that I will need a note to excuse his absence. Are you aware he is not in attendance?" There was a tremble of excitement in the woman's voice, as if she was thrilled that finally, among what was undoubtedly dozens of phone calls for delinquent teens, she'd caught one troublemaker red-handed.

"Ms. Farmer," he said, "I waved at him this morning when he left for school. He may have been a few minutes late, but I'm sure he's there." He tried to have faith in Colter. Sure, the kid had been acting out lately, but what sixteen-year-old didn't? Maybe the attendance secretary had it all wrong. Colter wouldn't have screwed up twice in two days.

"I assure you, Mr. Jensen, he has not arrived. His homeroom and first period teachers have reported him in absentia."

In absentia... If Colter had to deal with her type all day, it was no wonder he skipped class.

"I'll take care of it."

"I'm glad to hear it. As things stand, I will be marking him down as unexcused. Two more and he will be in considerable trouble."

"Don't worry. He's already in *considerable trouble*." He hung up the phone and turned back to his cooling eggs.

He couldn't just pick up and leave Elke now. She would run. He could see it in the way she kept glancing over at him as if she was the rabbit and he the hound. If he left now, it was likely he would never get answers.

He picked up his phone and dialed Colter.

"Hello?" Colter answered.

"Where in the hell are you?" He tried to ask quietly, but based on the wide eyes of the retirement-aged woman in the booth next to him, he'd failed.

"What?" Colter paused. "I'm at school."

"Then why did I just get a call from the attendance office?"

"That's bull. I'm here, Dad."

"Is that right? Then walk down to that office right now and let me talk to Ms. Farmer."

"But…Dad, I'm in the middle of a test."

"A test so important you answered your phone?" Kevin growled. "You better have your butt in Ms. Farmer's office in less than ten minutes." He hung up and glanced down at his watch. Elke didn't get off for another thirty minutes.

There was little to no chance Colter was at school, or would be at the school in ten minutes, but if Kevin left to check on him, he'd be putting his job and the investigation in danger. The parenting books always said he had to "be consistent" and "follow through." How was he expected to be consistent and follow through when he had a job that pulled him in an opposite direction?

He took a pull of his coffee. Colter was going to have to wait. This job paid the bills. This job was the only thing that held the family—or at least what was left of the family—together. Colter was acting impulsively and whether he meant to do it or not, he was pulling apart what little family they had left.

He thought about calling Heather, but after last night…he couldn't. Not with so many unspoken things between them. For all he knew, she hated him.

He had to go at this one alone. It was his job as a father to make sure he drew the family together.

If he hurried he could make it to the school and back to meet Elke in thirty minutes. That was, if Colter did as he was told.

Kevin stood up and pulled out his wallet. He went to grab a twenty to pay for breakfast but stopped. His cash was gone.

Damn that kid.

Elke brushed by him.

"Hold on a sec," he said. He couldn't lose track of Elke, if he did, he would miss his chance to find the perpetrator and he'd be back to square one. "I have to go, but you better be at that coffee shop or you will be suspect number one."

Chapter Eight

If Heather had been asked to describe a lawyer's office, this would have been the last thing she would have envisioned. The little room was hidden in an office building in the middle of downtown, seemingly content to disappear in mediocrity. The black melamine doorplate blended in with the shadows, barely making it possible to read the sign: Phyllis Kohl, Attorney at Law.

Everything about the place, from the hand-worn doors to the squeal of an unseen radiator, made Heather want to turn around and leave.

Everything she had tried to do for the past year had ended in failure; her marriage had crumbled and nearly all of her friendships had disappeared. She had even failed at her attempt to finally act on her feelings toward Kevin.

She tapped on the antique door.

"Hello?" a woman replied, her voice muffled as though she was in the middle of eating.

"Ms. Kohl? May I come in? It's Mrs. Sampson. I called earlier?"

There was a rustle of paper. "Yes. Come right in."

Heather opened the door and was met with the scent

of onion and liverwurst so strong that she stood outside until she could summon the will to continue.

A woman in her early twenties with stringy blond hair and a wrinkled black suit sat behind a desk covered in paperwork. A water cooler gurgled in the corner of the room and beside it a stack of paper cups and a box of tissues.

"Thanks for seeing me. I know this was short notice, but…well…"

Ms. Kohl dropped her lunch into her desk drawer. "I completely understand, Mrs. Sampson. These things have a way of sneaking up on us, don't they?"

Her divorce hadn't exactly snuck up on her. If she had been smarter, if she had paid more attention to the signs—the late nights, the terrible notes and the effort he had made not to touch her. No, this hadn't just snuck up on her; she'd just been too stupid to see it coming.

But now wasn't the time to argue.

There was only a single picture on the wall and it was a degree from the University of Montana Law School. The date at the bottom was last spring.

Ms. Kohl must have just passed the bar. She was probably full of hopes and dreams, and yet, she was just another victim to be taken down by Heather's husband.

Unfortunately, after calling law offices all morning, this newbie was all she could afford.

A lifetime of trying to please a man and all it had amounted to was a few thousand dollars and a crappy lawyer.

"Would you like to take a seat?" Ms. Kohl motioned toward the folding chair.

"Thanks." Heather sat down, the folding chair creaking as she moved. She tried not to notice the way the cheap seat cut into her legs. Comfort didn't matter. Nothing about what was going to happen in the next few hours would be comfortable.

"So you mentioned that your husband... Daryl?"

"David."

"Yes. *David.*" Ms. Kohl made a note on a napkin. "You said David has asked for a divorce. You mentioned you had a prenuptial agreement?"

Heather pulled the manila envelope out of her purse. "Here's the prenup and the documents he gave me. I signed it a few months before our wedding, seven years ago."

"That's great," Ms. Kohl said as she took the envelope. She pulled out the paperwork and scanned the pages. "It looks like he has gone ahead and already filed for the divorce." She flipped over the next page. "Everything seems pretty straightforward."

Only a new lawyer would have made the mistake of calling a divorce straightforward. Nothing about what was happening around her seemed to be clear-cut. Everything, from the way she brushed her teeth to the roads she drove, seemed hard to remember. Everything was fuzzy, as though a haze of emotion had engulfed her and clouded even her most mundane, habitual actions with a fog of confusion that had her questioning her sanity.

"He's accused me of having an affair. Will that affect our agreement?"

"Were you having an affair?" Ms. Kohl looked up at her. "Wait, let me rephrase that... Is there any direct *evidence* of you having an affair?"

"I've never cheated on my husband. So, no, there

can't be any evidence. But he's… Well, David doesn't let things go."

Ms. Kohl set the papers down on her desk and glanced at the prenuptial agreement. "You have some things in here that may protect you, but without having a closer look, it's hard for me to say exactly how much is going your way. However, one thing I am seeing is that it looks like you are on a vesting schedule."

"A vesting schedule?"

"Yes, you don't remember this being discussed before you signed?"

She didn't want to admit to the lawyer that she'd read the contract over with nothing more than a glass of wine and a desperate desire for marriage. She hadn't paid attention to too many details. At the time, David had been her lifeline, a heroic doctor coming to rescue her from her dysfunctional family in his white Porsche. He had made promises that he would never act like her father, who came and went as he pleased—not coming home at all some nights—and then demanded they revere him. It was a cycle of love and hate, emotional manipulation at its worst.

Then she had been daft enough to fall for David's promises—only to have him repeat the cycle. She had been so naive.

She'd trusted him and the promises he'd made. She'd trusted that the prenup he'd given to her was fair.

"Well, Mrs. Sampson, a vesting schedule is basically a division of assets based on the length and/or reproductive success of your marriage."

"Reproductive success?"

"Yes, basically you are given more money if you

have more children." Ms. Kohl looked up at her with a quizzical expression. "Do you have any children?"

"We tried. I lost one. On and off since then we've tried, but we haven't had any luck."

"Hmm…" She looked back at the paper. "What did your lawyer say when you signed this document?"

Heather chewed on her lip. "Uh, well, I didn't have a lawyer."

"You signed this without a lawyer's review?" Ms. Kohl's face was awash with horror. "You should never have signed this. Who knows what else he's snuck into the pages. I'm going to need a few hours to go over this."

What else could David have put into the agreement that would be worse than paying her for having children? It was as if she was nothing more than a brood mare—worse, an unsuccessful brood mare. Thanks to her poor reproduction ability, he was basically sending her off to the glue factory.

Without a fair settlement, she would have to go to work at a glue factory. Who else would want to hire a woman with only a high school education and a broken past?

She tried to swallow the lump that had formed in her throat. Now wasn't the time to cry.

"He'll pay me alimony, won't he?" Heather asked, her voice thick with poorly harnessed emotion.

"Hmm…" Ms. Kohl tapped her finger on the paper. "Here it says, basically, that you will be getting no alimony for any marriage that lasts less than fifteen years. However, based on the length of your marriage—seven years—you will get 15 percent of all assets accrued during the time you were married."

"What about premarital assets?"

"Whatever was achieved before marriage remains in the hands of the original owner and isn't to be split or taken into consideration in the calculation of assets accrued."

She and David owned three homes, but two he had bought the week before they were married. The sudden rush to buy homes had seemed strange, but he'd brushed her concern off by telling her it was all an investment. He'd failed to mention the investment was only for him.

The only house she had any right to, then, was the one in which they lived. Even then, it would only be 15 percent of the sale value. They were in debt on the home up to their eyeballs, maybe deeper, but she couldn't be sure. She hadn't seen their account in months. They had a man to do that. David had always kept her on an allowance—no more than five hundred dollars per month.

"So, I'm getting nothing?"

"Well, you will get the 15 percent," Ms. Kohl said in a reassuring tone.

There was no reassuring her.

"Here," Ms. Kohl said as she pointed at another sheet of paper from the envelope. "In the letter from his attorney, it says he's willing to give you the house and a settlement of ten thousand dollars. Does that sound like it's about 15 percent of your assets?"

Her throat tightened. "I have no idea."

Ms. Kohl's eyebrow rose. "You don't know?"

"I don't have access to our accounts. Well, *I did*, but I didn't have anything to do with them. I just gave him my receipts at the end of the month."

"It sounds like you've been a very trusting woman, Mrs. Sampson."

Yes, very trusting and, looking back, very stupid. Now her trust was coming back to bite her.

"What do I need to do?"

Ms. Kohl pressed her hands together and laid them on the desk. "Do you think you would be happy with the house and the ten thousand dollars?"

"I don't work. I wouldn't be able to afford to pay the mortgage on the house for more than a few months. And then there would be nothing left."

"What if we let him have the house? What if you just took the money? Maybe we could negotiate for more."

She shook her head. "I need alimony. At least until I can get on my feet. Maybe go back to school…" Or maybe even think about finding someone who wanted to have a future together, someone who loved her for exactly who she was—someone like Kevin.

"We can try." Ms. Kohl sighed. "But unless we can find a way to prove this contract is null and void, it's likely this will hold up in court."

David was going to leave her with nothing and with no way to live—all because of his crazy paranoia and the fact that she hadn't given him a child.

Ms. Kohl leaned forward. "Are you sure that this divorce is something you really want?"

Chapter Nine

"What were you thinking?" Kevin growled as Colter flopped down in the seat next to him in the attendance office.

"What?" Colter crossed his arms over his chest and slouched so low in the chair that his chin rested on his chest. "I'm here. Ain't I?"

"You just got here. Where were you?" Kevin whispered, he didn't want to draw the attention of Ms. Farmer, who was talking on the phone.

"I told you... I was here." Colter kicked his backpack as though the bag was proof he'd shown up to class.

"Don't treat me like I'm stupid. Your car wasn't in the parking lot. I had to walk out on an investigation to come and deal with this. The least you can do is tell me where you were."

Colter jumped to his feet. "I can't believe you're coming down on me like this. You're the one who doesn't show up."

Kevin stopped him. "You need to get to class." He looked his son in the eye. "Do I need to escort you there to make sure you make it?"

"I got it." Colter picked up his backpack and made his way out of the office.

"And get your butt home straight after school!" he called after him. "And the twenty dollars that's missing…it better find its way back into my wallet."

Kevin hated the way Colter stared at him, with contempt in his eyes. He'd always tried to do the best he could and now here he was in the seventh level of hell—frozen, unable to stop his son's self-destructive path the past few months. The worst thing was that he didn't understand why Colter was acting up.

Kevin stood up and walked to the secretary's desk, where she still jabbered away on the phone. "Please mark Colter Jensen as present." He motioned toward the door. "He's on his way to class."

The secretary nodded and hung up the phone. "I have a note here from Colter's baseball coach." She handed him a sealed envelope with *To the parent(s) of Colter Jensen* written across the front.

He took it and fled from the office. Getting to his truck, he stared down at the envelope but he couldn't open it.

He threw the letter on the dashboard.

Whatever the coach had to say could wait. All he could hope was that Colter's coach wasn't having the same problems he was with his son. Colter got decent grades, but his future hinged on his baseball. That would be his gateway to college, his chance to break away from Missoula and make something of himself. If he screwed this up, Kevin couldn't bail him out.

Their lives would be so much easier if only Colter's frontal lobe would just kick in and help him realize there were consequences to every decision.

Kevin snorted. *Consequences* were something he knew entirely too much about… After last night with

Heather, his own personal consequences were about to rain down.

His head ached. He would deal with those flare-ups later. Now, he needed to get back to work.

THE COFFEE SHOP was awash with sound as people sat talking and others tapped away on their computers. Kevin sat down at an empty table in the corner and nursed a coffee as he waited for Elke. Hopefully she would come. He hated that his investigation hinged on a woman he might never see again.

The door to the coffee shop opened. Elke looked around, her gaze moving from one patron to the next. As she spotted him, she balled her fists as if she was summoning her resolve to face him.

She stomped over. "I didn't like ya showin' up to my work like that. You don't know what they been sayin' all day." Elke plopped down on the seat beside him. "I bet I lost twenty bucks in tips 'cause of you."

"Sorry, I didn't mean to get in your way." That wasn't entirely true. He'd wanted to be a visible presence, to let her catch a glimpse of what her life would be like if she refused to help him. "I just need to ask you a few questions. Now that you're not in your home, it's tough to catch up with you. You have a cell phone number?"

She shook her head. "Those things are a waste of money. The people who want to talk to me, they know where I live—or at least where I normally live. How long is it gonna be before I can get back into my place?"

"That's all up to you, Ms. Goldstein."

"Whatcha mean?"

"The quicker you answer my questions, the faster I can let you back into your house. As it is, I'm going to have to keep it off-limits until my investigation is concluded."

"Well, I don't know nothin'." Elke shuffled in her seat, picked up the roll of silverware off the table and inspected the pieces. She went off on a long soliloquy about the silverware at Rudy's.

Kevin listened. Sometimes the best way to get a person to answer the questions he wanted to ask was to not ask them at all. Rather it was better to lead them to the answer he wanted without them knowing they were giving him information. People, especially those who were stressed, had a way of talking too much. They would go on and on, each time they spoke giving away a little more about themselves and what they knew. Patience was the key.

"How long have you been at Ruby's?"

"Goin' on ten years. I make real good tips. My regulars, they love me."

"You get along with everyone you work with?"

"Yeah. Ain't got no problems. But mostly everyone keeps themselves to themselves—except the cooks. Those cooks are hornier than a rooster in a henhouse. You should hear some of the things they say." Elke frowned and shook her head as if she was appalled, but the gleam in her eye told him she enjoyed the cooks' lewd attentions.

"Dating any of them?"

"God, no." She laid the silverware on the table as a waitress stopped beside their table.

She ordered coffee.

"So you are dating?" Kevin asked, leading Elke back to the conversation once the waitress walked away.

"I'm always dating. Haven't found the right one yet.

Seems whenever I start gettin' to like a man he up and disappears. Ah well, that's life, right?" Elke looked at him as though she hoped he would lift her out of her endless cycle of dating.

An image of Heather flitted into his mind. He wouldn't mind dating her. He roped in his errant thoughts and focused on his investigation. "Would you say your relationships have dissipated or have some ended on a more tumultuous note?"

"Tumultuous note?" Elke gave him a confused look.

"I mean is there a man or anyone else upset with you?"

"I've never been good at pleasin' everyone."

"Was the man at your house the morning of the fire someone who wasn't pleased?"

Elke smiled and leaned in. "Oh, he was pleased."

"Was he?" Kevin asked, trying to hold back his excitement that he'd finally gotten her to admit there had been a man at her home. She'd fallen for the chatting trap.

"This old dog has learned a lot of tricks over the years." She leaned back, folding her arms proudly over her chest. "I'm not popular with the men for no reason."

"I just thought it was your good looks that had them coming around," Kevin said, playing into her flirtation.

Elke giggled.

The waitress walked to their table and set down a cup of coffee. "Anything else I can get you?"

"No," Elke said, shaking her head.

"Okay, well let me know if you need anything else." The girl smiled and left.

"She shoulda brought you a refill. It woulda saved her a trip." Elke pointed at his half-drained cup. "The young ones never understand that ya gotta work smart in this business. You need to save your energy for when you get home." She winked.

Kevin laughed. "I bet *your friend*—" he paused, hoping she would say the man's name, but she didn't take the bait "—appreciates your conservation of energy."

Elke laughed, her sound the coarse warble of a smoker. "You better believe it."

"What did you say his name was?"

"Anthony."

"And his last name?"

Elke chewed on the corner of her lip as if she was trying to remember. "I don't know. I don't think he ever said."

"So I'm guessing you hadn't been together long?"

She shook her head. "That was the first time I had him over. He'd come to Rudy's for dinner and ended up gettin' a little dessert."

"Do you think he was behind the fire?"

Elke took a long drink of her coffee. "In my line of work ya get to know people. I can tell you before a person sits down whether or not they are gonna stiff me or leave me a tip worth savin'. Do you think I would bring home a man who would start my stuff on fire? I work hard for my money."

She may have learned to read people in her business, but Kevin had, as well. And the first thing he'd learned about people is that given the right circumstances— most often need and opportunity—people were capable of anything.

"Can you describe him?"

She stared up at the ceiling. "Well, he was pretty average."

"Age? Hair, eye color?"

"He never said how old he was, but if I had to guess he was about forty, maybe forty-five. Dark hair. Brown eyes. Strong. Lean. Said he liked to work out."

Kevin thought back to the report. The neighbor had said the man coming out of the house in the morning had dark hair and an average build. It was possible this Anthony was the man they had seen, but at the same time, it was possible that it wasn't.

"Do you know where he works?"

"He never said. He's just been coming around the restaurant pretty regular. Always leaving me a twenty. A twenty five days a week can make a big difference."

"So you took him home to thank him personally?" Kevin asked, being careful to ask in a way that didn't ring of judgment.

Elke smiled. "I bet that's how you work. You help a woman and then end up taking her home."

Elke was wrong. His mind shifted to Heather, the last woman he'd taken home. No, he corrected himself, she'd come to him on her own. Still, he'd done nothing to help her; instead, he'd made her a victim of embarrassment by stopping her come-on. If only she hadn't been drunk… He could have finally done what he'd always wanted. He could have shown her what she was missing with David. He could make her feel how she deserved to feel.

If her reasoning hadn't been compromised, he wouldn't have stopped. Rather, he would have made the move; he would have taken her in his arms and kissed the curves of her lips, pulled her hips against him and caressed her over her clothes until she begged for his soft touch in more forbidden places.

He shook away the images.

"This conversation isn't about my dating history, Ms. Goldstein," Kevin said, trying to turn their conversation back to the business at hand.

"You might try to tell yourself that, but I know it ain't true. Everything we do in this world is pushed by our relationships—past and present. Who you are now is because of the people who've hated or loved you."

"I'm a professional inspector, ma'am. My investigations are based on science not on emotion."

Elke smirked. "Even for a man like you, everything comes back to feelings."

"Feelings can be the basis for many things, Ms. Goldstein, but an investigation isn't one of them." He readjusted the sleeves of his uniform. "Now, would you say Anthony left with particular *feelings* that would give him a motive for starting this fire?"

"Not that I know of." Elke shrugged.

"Did he spend the night?"

"I'm not the kind for sleepovers."

"So what time did he leave?"

She swirled the spoon in her coffee. "I don't know. I wasn't looking at my watch, but I would say sometime around two." She sipped her coffee. "And I ain't seen him again."

Things didn't align. The fire wasn't reported until 5:00 a.m. If the man left her house around two it either wasn't the same man the neighbors had seen or he had come back. Only one thing was for sure, he had one hell of an investigation on his hands.

Chapter Ten

Heather sat in her car as the tears flowed. They streaked down her face and her nose ran, but she let the ugly sobs take over. David was a jerk.

How could he have done this to her? She had given him everything—her life, her future, her heart.

What had he given her? Shame. Embarrassment. Regret.

She hated him for that. Despite that, her lawyer had pushed for her to reconsider the divorce—as if she had a choice. David was running this decision, just like he ran everything else.

She slammed her hand against the steering wheel, driving pain through her palm, but it was nothing compared to the pain in her soul.

What was she going to do?

She dabbed at her tears. She looked out the window. Around her, the city flowed like a river as people rushed through their lives.

Her eyes lit on a woman in the crosswalk, waiting until it was safe to cross. A little boy held her hand and under his arm was a blue bunny. The bunny's ears were gray, bits of a black gooey substance stained its fur, and its black plastic nose was askew. The boy's arm relaxed and the bunny dropped to the ground as the boy's mother tugged on his hand, urging him to come along as she crossed the street.

The boy's eyes widened and he dropped to his knees, protesting about his lost friend. His mother spotted the toy and, gathering the boy in her arms, retrieved the bunny. The boy pulled his toy tight under his arm, protecting it with the strength of his love.

A renewed wave of tears flooded Heather's cheeks. What it must be like to be loved like the bunny, to be wanted regardless of the dirt on its ears and the wear on its fur. What she would give to be loved like that… especially by a child.

She would give anything to have that moment. To be given the gift of motherhood. To be able to pull a child into her arms and fix all the wrongs with a simple kiss. To love wholeheartedly without the fear of being abandoned. Or to know the child in your arms loved you with every thread of their being.

It wasn't just her vanity that made her want a family. No. It was so much more. It was a deep ache in her gut, a feeling in her core every time she thought of a child. Like an amputee felt a lost phantom limb, she felt the loss of her child, who had never had a chance to exist more than a few weeks in her inhospitable womb.

Every ounce of her love had ended in loss.

Heather sobbed as the mother and her boy made their way across the street.

What she would have given to still have her mother around. Her mother had been tough, but she'd always been there. It was in moments like these when she missed her the most. She missed everything about her, from the way her hair always smelled like hair spray to the way she would wrap her arms around her and tell her the things she needed to hear. Alone, she wasn't strong enough to make it through. She would never make it through to the other side.

She would prove a broken heart could be fatal.

She needed a friend.

Heather drew her phone out of her purse and stared at the screen. Kevin's face greeted her as she looked at her recent calls. God, she wished she could call him. To confide in him what the lawyer had told her. It would have felt so good to be back in his arms, listening to the soothing beat of his heart, to feel the strong touch of his lips.

She'd stepped too far over the boundary of friendship. He had pushed her away. If he felt as she did, he wouldn't have been able to stop.

She needed to talk to someone neutral. Looking to her phone, the only other two people on her recent calls list were David and Brittany. She clicked on Brittany and the call went through.

"Are you busy?" she asked when her friend answered.

There was a short pause. "Um… No. What's up?"

"David wants a divorce."

"What?" There was an odd strain in Brittany's voice.

Heather couldn't bring herself to repeat the words and the phone crackled and buzzed with the silence between them.

"Where are you?" Brittany asked.

"I'm outside my lawyer's office."

"So you already went to see someone. That's good. Has David filed anything yet?"

"He had the papers ready last night."

"Damn. I didn't think he was going to do this so fast."

"What? You knew he was going to ask for a divorce?"

There was a long pause. "Well, no. But things have been so rocky with you guys. I thought maybe it was possible he would pull something stupid like this."

The word *stupid* didn't seem to cut it. This was more than stupid. It was irrational, terrifying and horrific. More, it was life shattering.

Her mind was a muddled mess of thoughts, like a painting that she was standing too close to so that the colors streaked in no discernible order. Unlike the painting, however, she doubted that if she stepped back she could make sense of the mess in her life. There was no beautiful picture, no passion behind the madness.

"Heather?"

"Huh?"

"Why don't you come over?"

"Okay," she said, her body numb.

She drove on instinct, bobbing and weaving through traffic and turning down the streets that she had driven a thousand times. She pulled into Brittany's driveway where, only yesterday, she'd come to celebrate. The pink metallic party streamers were still hanging on the porch and they fluttered in the breeze as though they were beckoning party-goers. In her, they would find only disappointment.

Heather made her way up to the streamers and, without thinking, reached up and pulled them down. The wispy foil crinkled in her hands as she balled it up in her fist.

"Hey now, they didn't do anything to you," Brittany said as she opened the door and motioned her inside.

"I just thought—"

Brittany stopped her with a wave of her hand. "No worries. They needed to come down anyway. I'm just glad you're here."

False felicities. Women spoke in them all the time, offering a kind word and a smile when inside they were thanking God that something wasn't happening to them or, worse, snickering at their friend's misfortune as though it was some kind of karmic retribution.

Heather was just as guilty as the rest. She'd lost count of the number of times she had congratulated a pregnant woman with a fist in her gut. Now Brittany was welcoming her with the same double-edged greeting. No one wanted to spend their day with a blubbering mess. Brittany was just trying to do what she thought was right, but the strain in her smile spoke louder than her words.

"Thanks for having me. I didn't bring your clothes back. I'm afraid your shirt got a bit ruined, but I'll make sure—"

Another wave. "Don't worry about those silly old clothes. Just throw them away."

Heather nodded. Of course Brittany didn't want them back—they were not only tainted with last night's margaritas, they were also tainted with failure, and failure wasn't a going commodity in her world.

Heather shook her head to try to squash her thoughts. *She's trying to help. Why can't I just appreciate it? Why can't I just let her love me like a sister? Not everyone is out to get me.*

"Come on," Brittany said, motioning her toward the kitchen. "I have a cup of coffee waiting. I even put in the creamer you like." She sent Heather a smile.

Brittany handed her a fresh cup of coffee, the white cream billowing and swirling like a cloud of sweetness.

"Thanks. I appreciate your having me over. I know you've got better things to do."

"Stop it. You know I've got your back." Brittany walked to the other side of her granite island and poured herself a cup of coffee. "Why didn't you come over last night?"

Heather smiled as she thought of where, and with whom, she'd spent last night, and she tried to cover her reaction by taking a long drink.

She couldn't tell Brittany about Kevin. It wasn't that Brittany wouldn't understand; no, she would slap her back and praise her for her ability to go after the man she really wanted. Brittany had been through more than one breakup before settling down with Nathan. Every time her heart had been broken, she always landed on her feet—and in the bed of the next man. The same couldn't be said of her.

"You know I'm here," Brittany continued. "If you ever need me, you just have to call."

"I tried, but you didn't answer. With your party and all, you had enough going on. I didn't want to bother you."

"I can't believe you didn't come over. I mean I get it if you didn't feel like talking, but you could've at least slept in my guest room. You didn't have to be alone."

I wasn't alone. She bit back the words.

Heather looked around and tried to focus her attention on anything other than the pain and guilt that roiled within her. "Where's Nathan? He at work?"

"It's Friday, remember?"

"Oh…"

In truth, she had forgotten this was Nathan's day off.

Brittany smiled. "He needed to get out of the house. This is his golf morning. Afterward he normally hits the nineteenth hole. Most of the time he doesn't come home until dinner, and sometimes not even then. It's great. We both get a break."

"A break? Is everything going okay?"

Brittany nodded, maybe a bit too fervently. "Absolutely. But you know how it is." She smiled. "Absence makes the heart grow fonder."

Heather stared down at the mug in her hands. The white rim was stained with her pink lipstick, lipstick she didn't remember putting on.

"Maybe somehow your hiccup will end up helping," Brittany continued. "Maybe you guys just need a little break. Maybe he'll come around and see what a wonderful woman you are."

"I'm not wonderful."

"Stop that, Heather. You are. What other woman would do what you do for David?"

"I'm hardly the first woman to take care of the household." Heather looked up. "You do the same thing for Nathan."

"Hardly. You're the perfect wife. Every day David comes home from work to a hot meal. *Your* house is always clean." Brittany motioned to piles of letters, empty paper plates and last night's red Solo cups that littered her counter. "You volunteer everywhere and you watch other people's kids. You're one step away from being Mrs. Cleaver. In fact, the only thing keeping you from being the picture of a 1950s super wife is that you don't bring David his slippers and paper."

"He doesn't like sweaty feet."

Brittany's face pulled into a disgusted pucker. "See? You even know *that* about your husband. I couldn't tell you anything about Nathan's feet other than he has short toes. Really short toes, actually. They're freakishly troll-like. They're even hairy."

Heather giggled as she imagined Nathan, the bra-shirt-wearing griller with hairy troll feet.

Brittany reached over and squeezed her hand, reassuring her. "Look, every marriage goes through a rough patch. It's normal, especially after everything you guys have gone through. Maybe you just need to take this time to figure out who you are and what you want."

She ran her thumb over the smooth glass of the coffee mug.

Her thoughts moved to Kevin and the spark she'd felt last night when his eyes had met hers. She hadn't felt that want, that raw desire for David in a long time. Yet, if she was the super wife Brittany claimed, she would have felt nothing. She would never even have found her way to Kevin's front steps.

She was far from perfect—especially if someone asked David. No doubt he wanted a woman who would come to him in the night, lips parted and body needing. In the bedroom, she had played the part of a dutiful wife, but even then the feelings hadn't come close to what she had always felt for Kevin.

"Don't take this the wrong way," Brittany continued. "But maybe you've been *too* good at being a wife."

Heather choked on her swig of coffee, coughing until she could get the liquid out of her lungs. Tears streamed from her eyes and she dabbed at them with a napkin.

"If I was that good, then why would he want to leave me?" Her voice was thick and rough.

"You made life too easy. People don't appreciate things they don't have to work for." Brittany sighed. "Think about it. David had to work to get everything he has. He may not admit it, but he loves the chase. He loves having to tear his way to the top to get what he wants."

A knot of jealousy and confusion tightened in Heather's gut as she stared at Brittany. Her friend seemed to know more about David and what he wanted than she did. Sure, Heather had talked about David a lot over the years of their friendship, but there seemed to be something more than hearsay or simple familiarity in the way Brittany spoke.

What was she thinking? There couldn't be... She flushed the thoughts from her head.

"Do you want the divorce?" Brittany continued.

The question sat in the air like a heavy cloud.

"The lawyer asked me the same thing. To be honest, Brit, the only thing I know for sure is that I don't want things to keep going as they are."

Brittany nodded, but for once didn't say anything.

"There's a prenup," Heather said, looking down at her hands. "As things stand, if I go through with the divorce, I get ten thousand dollars and the house."

"That's it?"

"I'm lucky if I'll get that. The last time we spoke, David threatened to take everything. He thinks I broke the conditions of the contract. My lawyer thinks I'm in the clear, but I don't have a whole lot of faith in her."

"What did you do?"

Heather paused. Did she really want to tell Brittany that David had caught her sneaking out of Kevin's house? Brittany was her friend, but she doubted she would believe she'd done nothing with the handsome Kevin. Over the years, they'd laughed and talked about what it would be like to be with a man like him, but it had been nothing more than girl talk—until now. All of a sudden, with the proclamation of divorce, all of those talks had a new weight.

"He's accusing me of all kinds of things," Heather said, carefully sidestepping what and who was really on her mind. "He's even accusing me of cheating on him with his coworker, Andrew."

"Andrew Bosche—the one who has the huge nose and the piggish eyes?"

"The one and only."

Brittany laughed. "You could do a lot better than Andrew. Why would he think you'd ever go for someone like that?"

Heather explained David's convoluted thoughts, all the time trying to stop her hands from shaking. "I swear, Brittany, I've never slept with another man."

"I know, sweetheart. David's just the jealous type." Brittany sat her coffee cup down on the island and ran her finger over the rim. "Don't take this the wrong way, but do you think that he's accusing you to take the heat off him?"

"I considered that, but I don't know."

"It's kind of classic. A cheater always accuses the innocent to make themselves feel better. If they're not the only one cheating, then what they're doing isn't so bad. They feel justified in having an affair."

Until recently she had never thought David was the type to cheat. He was a doctor—a man held to a higher moral code. He'd always made a point of telling her how much his reputation mattered and reminding her that how she acted mattered. She had to be a good, upstanding wife so that he could appear to have the perfect life.

She had never let him down. At least not in her mind… That was, until last night when she'd kissed Kevin.

Instead of regret, empowerment flowed through her.

If what Brittany was saying was true, David was the one to blame. He was the one who was stripping down their marriage, leaving behind only tired flesh and fragile bones.

Right now, the dying beast wasn't worth saving.

"I'm sorry, Heather. I didn't mean to upset you. It's just… I just feel so bad seeing you go through this. You don't deserve this."

"It doesn't matter what I deserve. I just want—"

The front door slammed, rattling the lights in the kitchen and stopping Heather midsentence.

"What was that?" Heather jumped to her feet. "Was someone here?"

Brittany stood up. "No." She rushed out of the kitchen toward the door, Heather close behind. "Hello?"

There was nobody at the door, but the curtain on the window was drifting back into place. Brittany opened the door and they looked outside. The front yard was empty and everything stood still.

"What in the hell?" Brittany turned back to her. "Did you see anyone?"

She shook her head.

The faint aroma of chlorine stung her nostrils. "Are you bleaching something?"

"Huh? No." Brittany frowned. "Why?"

Heather sniffed, pulling the scent deeper into her

nose as she tried to follow the smell. She walked toward the stairs to the second floor.

A white haze filled the stairwell. It billowed and roiled as it hit the ceiling and started pouring downward. A tongue of orange flame wrapped around the wall at the top of the stairs. It spread, its blue maw stretching and gaping upward in its ravenous consumption of oxygen.

For a moment, she just stood staring as the orange tips rippled over the ceiling. In a disturbing but primal way, the fire was beautiful.

Heather forced herself to turn away. As she moved, something stirred behind the back window. A man stood staring at her, his face hidden in darkness. As quickly as she noticed him, the dark-haired man disappeared.

Brittany stepped around her and looked upward.

She screamed.

She tugged at Heather's arm, tearing her from her trance. "Heather, let's go!"

Stumbling through the door and out into the front yard, Heather couldn't help but emit a low, joyless laugh. She had come here for comfort, to see a friend and talk, yet no matter where she went, she left only destruction.

Chapter Eleven

Kevin sank back into the turquoise patio chair as the little boy ran across the porch and down the stairs, his plump little feet pounding on the wood as if he was beating a drum. The scent of smoke lingered in the air and strengthened as the wind drifted from the direction of Elke's house next door.

For a moment it was as though he had gone back in time and was watching Colter. Maybe if he tried hard enough he could look over to the neighbor's house and see Heather in the window. He smiled at the thought, Heather looking out at him…the feel of her against his body.

The door slammed behind him.

"Mr. Jensen, I'm surprised you're here. I thought they, you know…the investigators, were done questioning me," the blonde said, but her body language was soft and welcoming in direct incongruity with her words.

"I am sorry for the intrusion, Miss…" He looked down at his notes, searching for the woman's last name.

"Mrs. Jones. Tracy." She looked toward her son. "And he's River."

"River? Cool name." Kevin smiled. "I have two kids of my own. They grow quick, don't they?"

She nodded.

"How old is River?"

"He's two, and full of piss and vinegar, just like his father." Mrs. Jones smiled, pride lighting her eyes.

"What does his father—your husband—do?"

"He works for the railroad. Lays rail."

"Was he home the morning of the fire?"

Mrs. Jones glanced over at the house next door as though she was recalling everything that had happened. "Yeah, he gets up early for work. Most of the time he's out of the house by five. He's the one who noticed something was wrong."

Kevin took out his notepad and made a note. "Do you know what he saw?"

"At first he noticed the smoke, and then he came upstairs and woke me up. By the time I made it out of bed and to the window, there was a man standing on the front porch."

"Are you sure it was a man? Did you see his face?"

"I had been up most of the night with River, so I was pretty tired, but I'm pretty sure it was a man." Mrs. Jones sat down in the patio chair next to him as she carefully kept a watch on River. who was playing with a yellow truck in the grass. "I didn't catch his face, but it was too big to be a woman, and he had dark hair, short, cropped."

"Was it dark outside when you caught sight of this man?"

"Yeah. It was dark at five. But Elke's porch light was on."

River roared, mimicking the sound of a dump truck's engine.

"How well do you know Elke?"

"Mostly in passing. She keeps different hours than us, so our relationship pretty much consists of waving."

They sounded like typical neighbors. "You don't have any animosity toward Ms. Goldstein?"

"Nah," Mrs. Jones said, waving him off. "We get along. She's even offered to watch River for me." Her face tightened. "You don't think what happened over there will continue happening, do you?"

"You mean arson?" Kevin asked.

"Well, yeah. You don't think we're in danger, do you?" She looked worriedly toward River, her fingers gripping the edge of her patio chair.

"No, ma'am." He tried to sound reassuring, but if she had been listening well, she would have been able to hear the lie in his voice. The truth was that he didn't know who was behind the fire. Elke had been helpful, but he wasn't any closer to finding the person responsible. He could only hope he'd been wrong about this arsonist being one who would strike again.

There was a long pause as he tried to think of something reassuring to say to the mother.

Mrs. Jones looked at him. "Oh, I just remembered something..."

"What?"

"The man wasn't driving. I remember him walking off, down the side of the road, and I thought it was strange. I mean, what grown man doesn't have a car?" Her face pinched.

Kevin made a note: No getaway vehicle.

That could mean one of several things. Maybe the man had planned to set the fire and didn't want to be easily identifiable. Or maybe the man didn't have a car.

Could he have been a transient? Missoula was known for having a sizable population of homeless people.

"Did you see what the man was wearing?"

She closed her eyes like she was trying to recall a memory. "I think he was wearing black pants. And he had on a T-shirt. White."

"Did the T-shirt have any logos on it? Any identifiable features?"

She shook her head. "I don't remember. Like I said, I was pretty tired. He had on hiking boots, though. You know, like the ones that loggers wear."

Kevin made another note. He thought back to the footprint he'd seen in Elke's garage. It had been made by a boot with a star pattern. That had to belong to his suspect. Finally a lead, but it wasn't much.

"How old would you say the man looked?"

"I don't know. It was hard to tell."

"Did he look to be in his forties?"

Mrs. Jones bit her lip. "Maybe, I didn't really get a chance to look too closely at his face. For all I know, he could have been a twentysomething or he could have been fifty. He was a little heavy, though. Kind of a paunch belly."

Elke had described Anthony as being in his midforties with a trim build. This man, the man Tracy was describing, didn't fit the description.

He needed to question Anthony, but it suddenly seemed unlikely he was the man who'd set the fires.

Did the possible arsonist see Anthony coming out of her house and get jealous? Could it have been one of Elke's former lovers?

From what Elke had said, there were plenty of them.

But he knew he couldn't jump to assumptions. He had to follow the evidence—regardless of how little there was.

There was a crash of two plastic trucks hitting one another and River making the sound effects of some poor imaginary victim.

"Is there anything else you or your husband noticed? Anything at all?"

She gave him a tired look. "I told you everything."

"Sorry, just trying to get as many facts as I can. I appreciate your patience in aiding with our investigation."

"Isn't there something you can do? You know, some CSI stuff?"

Kevin smiled. Mrs. Jones had an idealized vision of what power he wielded. He didn't live on the set of *NCIS* or whatever crime-drama television show she watched after River went to bed. He worked on a shoestring budget, where even having men maintaining the chain of custody was a cost his department didn't want to absorb.

He imagined taking the request to the crime lab to run shoe prints for a simple arson with no fatalities. If the chief heard about something like that, he would be canned for sure.

His phone rang, "Eye of the Tiger" sounding from his pocket. His thoughts instantly turned to Heather. "Excuse me," he said to Tracy.

"Hello?" he answered, hoping to hear Heather's voice.

"Kevin, this is Hiller. You busy?" the battalion chief asked.

"Well, actually, I'm in the middle of questioning a witness. What can I do for you?" He smiled over at Mrs. Jones who, nodding, stood up and made her way down the patio steps and to River's side.

"We are on another call. Upper Miller Creek. We have another fire you might want to look at."

He wasn't going to be able to continue his investigation on this fire if he was chasing after another one. If he walked away, the chain of custody would be broken and, if he returned, any evidence he found would make the case harder to prosecute. He'd promised himself he'd help Elke and that he'd find an answer. It wasn't just a simple investigation anymore. It had morphed into something else the moment he'd first seen River, the little boy who reminded him so much of Colter. What happened if this arsonist was targeting this block? What if the boy was in danger? He couldn't let the boy be hurt.

He couldn't stand the thought of someone getting hurt at the arsonist's hands; he'd seen too much pain between Allison's death and the multitude of cases he had investigated. This was one case where, if he just worked hard enough, if he just dug deeper, he'd find the answers he needed. If he just did his best, maybe he'd have the power to save a life.

"Isn't there someone else who can take that one? I have my hands full," Kevin said, trying to think of another, more urgent reason for him to refuse to bow out and leave this case unsolved.

"Actually, that's why I called," Hiller said. "This fire looks as if it may be tied to the other. We have what looks to be the same oxidizers used, but it's hard to say for sure."

He knew it. He knew another fire would happen. He'd failed.

"Was anyone hurt?" He braced himself for the answer.

"Two women were in the residence at the time of the

fire, but they made it out unharmed." There was a line of tension in his voice.

"What aren't you telling me, Hiller?"

Hiller cleared his throat. "Well, Jensen, they asked for you. Said they're friends of yours."

There was the echo of feminine voices on Hiller's end. "Hold on, ladies. I'll let him know." Hiller sighed with annoyance. "It's a Brittany Miller and her friend Heather Sampson."

Heather and Brittany?

Hiller had to be kidding.

"They're both okay? How's Heather?"

Hiller chuckled. "They're both fine. Including Heather."

Thank God she hadn't been hurt. After what had happened between them, he would have never forgiven himself.

"Where was the fire?"

Hiller rattled off Brittany's house number. A sense of relief drifted through him—at least it wasn't Heather's house.

"I'll be there in fifteen minutes."

KEVIN PARKED ACROSS the street from Brittany's two-story house. He looked over the mass of trees and lights that was the city below. Most days he would have enjoyed the hillside view, but right now all he could think of was Heather.

Heather. He shouldn't have been so worried about Heather. She couldn't be his. No matter how much he longed to kiss her pink lips, feel her warmth pressed against his body.

She had been so warm...

Damn it. Knock it off, Jensen.

Two fire engines and the battalion chief's truck were parked in front of Brittany's house where, only yesterday, he'd suffered through her annual neighborhood party. The only bright spot of the barbecue had been seeing Heather walk out of Brittany's house in her sexy miniskirt and low-cut top. He needed to write to whoever invented that shirt a thank-you; seeing her in that top was one image he would never forget—no matter how much he should.

Hiller was standing over by his crew, directing them in their attack on the smoldering blaze.

His breath hitched for a second as Heather stepped out from behind the ambulance. Ash smudged her cheeks and her eyes were shadowed with what he could only assume was fear. Even frazzled, she was beautiful.

Kevin made his way over to her. "Are you okay?"

She turned toward him and, before he had time to react, she threw her body into his arms, pressing hard against him. Her hair smelled of acrid smoke, but underneath the pungent smell was the heady floral aroma of her shampoo. Something about the smell, the safe beneath the dangerous, made some of his concern for her dissolve. She would be okay. She would make it through this. She hadn't been physically hurt. Only the memories of this would remain.

"You sure you're okay?" Kevin asked again, leaning back so he could look her in the face.

She nodded. "Fine. I...I'm sorry about last night. I—"

He stopped her with a shake of his head. "Don't worry. Let's not talk about it here." As he said the words, he instantly regretted them. He didn't want to forget what had happened between them—or at least what had almost happened—and he didn't want her to, either.

They both just needed time. And she needed time to figure out what was going on with her life.

She let her arms drop from his waist and the cool evening air robbed him of her warmth. The hard edges returned to her face and she stepped back from him.

He tried not to notice the way her body, which had only seconds before been open to him, closed.

"What happened?" he asked her. "Where's Brittany?"

"Don't worry. Brittany's fine. She's just getting checked out by the EMTs." Heather looked toward the ambulance. "As for what happened, I don't understand it. We were standing around in the kitchen, talking. Then we heard the front door slam. Then the smoke started pouring from the second floor."

Another second-floor fire and perhaps another fire started with an oxidizer. Assuming it was the same type of ignition source, it had to be the same arsonist. But why was this man starting all the fires on the second floor? Why not where they would be more deadly? Why not the kitchen or somewhere he could easily get away from?

Whoever had set the fire must have known Heather and Brittany were in the house. If he'd wanted them dead, he would have never started the fire in a place where it was unlikely to trap them. If he'd wanted to hurt Brittany and Heather, he would have set a hotter, more explosive fire at escape points.

Just like Elke's, this fire wasn't set to hurt. No. It

was set to send a message. But what did Brittany and Elke have in common?

"Is that where Brittany's bedroom is?" He pointed toward the second-story window above the front door.

"Huh?"

"Is her bedroom on the second floor? Near where the fire was started?"

"That's her bedroom, but I don't know exactly where the fire started. We never went up there. We just saw the smoke." Her eyes clouded over, as if she was suddenly gripped by thought. "When I turned I think I saw a man looking in the window."

"What? What did he look like?"

"I don't know." She shook her head. "He was in shadows."

"Anything you remember about him, anything at all?"

"He...he had dark hair. I couldn't see his face. But I could feel him watching me." Heather hugged her body. "Kevin... I have a feeling this guy isn't done."

He moved to hold her, but stopped as Hiller looked over toward them. "Don't worry, Heather. If I have my way, this will all be over soon. I won't let anything happen to you."

Chapter Twelve

She shouldn't have allowed herself to run into Kevin's arms...not after last night. Then again, he had taken her willingly. Maybe she was seeing things that weren't there, but she could have sworn he hadn't wanted to let her go.

Heather collapsed onto the grass of Brittany's front yard, which was wet where the firemen had sprayed water, quickly dousing the flames.

The fire hadn't been huge, but thanks to the phalanx of firefighters, EMTs and neighbors, it had blown into a full-scale event. Even the news crews had arrived, and the perky brunette from the ten o'clock news was interviewing neighbors.

Kevin was talking to a man he'd introduced to her as Stephen Hiller, his battalion chief. As he spoke, Kevin kept looking over and giving her reassuring smiles.

She was so confused. All she should have been thinking about was the fire and her burned-out marriage. Instead, all she could think about was the way it had felt to be in Kevin's arms.

After last night, she had convinced herself she wouldn't let it happen again, that she wouldn't let herself run to him. Yet she had allowed herself to fall into the arms of her hero.

That's exactly what he was—a hero.

It had nothing to do with the fact that he was a firefighter. Not anymore. No. He was so much more. He had such a good heart. There had been so many little things he done over the years, moments of selflessness, that showed her how much he cared. Once when she'd been sick, he had shown up with a bowl of chicken noodle soup. After she had lost the baby, he had the kids bring her flowers as a reminder that they loved her, that they would all be there.

He was so different from David. In fact, he was exactly the opposite of her narcissistic, demeaning, jerk of a husband.

She slapped her hands over her mouth as though she'd said the words aloud, though no sound had escaped her lips.

She hadn't meant that.

David wasn't a bad man. There had been a point early in their marriage when he'd been the picture of the perfect husband—bringing her flowers, coming home early and telling her every spare minute how much he loved her—but time had passed and it had all changed. As the months and years passed, the nice side of him had slipped away, only returning when they were in the presence of others. At home, she'd been left with nothing but the hatred and bitter, angry words that he kept hidden from the outside world.

There was no fixing things. There was no going back. There was only moving forward.

Maybe that was why they had never been given the

gift of children. In fact, maybe it was a message that they should never have been together.

Brittany's impish laugh cut through the air from the direction of the ambulance. Heather looked over at her friend, who even in the face of destruction was smiling as if she was on stage at the Miss America Pageant. She touched the arm of the twentysomething EMT and tilted her head back with another hearty laugh.

She wished she could be more like Brittany, beautiful and majestic even in moments of turmoil.

Kevin made his way over to her. A large black bag was draped over his shoulder. It was unzipped and inside were empty evidence bags. "Still doing okay? Do you need something?"

She needed a lot of things. First, she wanted to escape the spotlight. She hated this—this sideshow for the public. She didn't want her life, or even her day, to be scrutinized. She just wanted to go home and bury her head in a pillow or, better yet, to climb into Kevin's warm arms and forget everything.

"I'm fine," she lied, staring at Kevin's biceps, which pulled hard against his white uniform shirt. His badge sparkled in the sunshine, drawing her gaze to his chest.

"Before I wrap up here, are you feeling up to a couple more questions?"

Heather nodded even though all she really wanted to do was escape.

"Did you see anyone parked outside at any point during your visit?"

Heather thought about the moment she'd pulled up to the house. "I don't think so. Then again, I wasn't really paying attention. I had my mind on..." She paused as she thought about the last time she saw him.

"I completely understand," he said, a soft knowing smile on his face. "I—" He stopped and looked down at his notes.

What had he intended to say? What had he held back?

She warmed as she imagined him telling her that he had been just as torn about their night together or, rather, their almost night together. More than likely, however, he was thinking about a way to do his job and help her once again.

She thought of what it meant to be a true hero. It wasn't someone who ran into a burning building; a sociopath could do that. Rather, a hero was someone with great fears. They were the ones who feared the fire, who had dreams of the heat and woke up smelling imaginary smoke, yet who each day ran into those buildings, compelled by the need to help and refusing to be beaten by nightmares. In an odd way it made her think of the battle she faced. If only she could refuse to be beaten.

He smiled as she looked him in the eyes, and she could have sworn she caught a glimpse of his heart. This hard, battle-worn hero had turned gentle, made himself vulnerable, all for her. Whatever he had held back from saying didn't matter.

Kevin shifted from one foot to the other, looking away. "Did you see anyone near the house, other than when you saw him at the window?"

"I wish I could help you more, but all I saw was the shadow of a man." She shook her head. "We had no idea anyone was in the house with us. I don't even know why anyone would want to hurt Brittany."

"Do you think someone would want to hurt *you*?" He glanced in the direction of her and David's house.

She swallowed the gasp that lodged in her throat. "You don't think David would want to hurt me, do you?"

Kevin looked up, worry in his eyes. "Is there anything he has said or done to make you think he would target you in this type of act?"

"He's said so many things." There was a quake in her voice. "Lately, the things he's been doing to me have come as a surprise. I never thought he would hurt me like he has."

"He—" Kevin stopped. "Has he hurt you *physically*?"

She shook her head. "He's done a lot of things, but he's never raised a hand."

Kevin nodded, a frown darkening his face. "Are you afraid to go home?"

If she told Kevin the truth, that she was afraid, there would be no going back to the way things were. Undoubtedly, David would be moved up on Kevin's list of suspects. He would be questioned. No doubt he would quickly realize why he'd been put there and he would be even angrier.

If she told Kevin the truth, her world would be forever changed.

"I don't want to go back home."

"Do you have somewhere to go? Somewhere that you'll feel safe?"

She only had Brittany and Kevin.

"I'll just go back. Maybe he's gone."

"You need to stay away. Let me figure out what's going on. Maybe he's nothing to worry about, but maybe he is. I don't want you walking into a hornet's nest."

Everything with David was a hornet's nest.

"Okay. I'll look into getting a hotel room or something."

"Do you have any cash? You can't pay with a credit card. If you do, he can easily find out where you are."

She hated to admit how little money she had access to. For all she knew, David had already cancelled her credit and debit cards. Her stomach lurched at the thought.

Kevin reached out toward her. "Are you okay? You look pale. Why don't you sit down?" He motioned to the ambulance.

She shook her head. She would be fine; she just wasn't used to her world crashing down on her.

"I need to get some cash."

"You haven't done that yet?" He frowned. "You're a trusting woman. I know more than a few spouses who made it a personal mission to clear out bank accounts when they were planning a divorce."

The blood rushed from her head.

"Are you okay?" Kevin asked.

"I'm fine…" In truth, she was numb.

Kevin motioned toward the battalion chief. "Hiller, you can pull your men off Elke's house. I need them here instead. Got it?"

Hiller's face puckered. "I told you—" He stopped midsentence as he looked toward Heather. "Fine. Twelve hours, Jensen. But that's it."

There was a wave of tension between the two men, making Heather wish she was anywhere other than standing between them.

"Fine," Kevin said.

Hiller spun on his heel and yelled at one of the firefighters who stood near Brittany's front door.

Kevin turned to her. "I'll take you to the bank."

"You can't do that. You have to stay here and finish your investigation."

"I can take a short break." He looked back at the house and his face went rigid.

She was interfering in his work.

"Thanks for the offer. Really. But this is something I'm going to have to do on my own." She thought about how she would react if David had robbed her of everything. Kevin didn't need to see her sink any lower. "Would you just let Brittany know where I've gone?"

"No problem. By the way, I have an extra bedroom. It even has a lock on the door." He tensed. "I mean, if you don't want to get a hotel. I could use the help. I would pay you to take care of the kids."

She was tempted to take him up on his offer, but she shook her head. No matter how much she dreamed of a life with him, dreams rarely became reality.

In all of Kevin's studies, the motives for arson varied from revenge to fraud to some sociopathic impulse, and the list went on and on, but serial cases were different. Serial arsonists lived for the thrill. They reveled in the strike of the match, the smell of the smoke and the feel of power and control when they watched a fire ignite. Many serial arsonists were proud of their work—and that pride was what often got them caught. Many returned to the scene of the crime hours, days or weeks after the crimes just to see their devastation.

Kevin couldn't wait for that pride to get his perp caught.

Now that things had quieted down, he wanted one more chance to get a look at the scene. It was easy to miss something in the rush of firefighters—and it was easy to lose evidence. He'd given up the chain of custody at Elke's, so Brittany's was his only chance.

With a stiff nod he acknowledged the rookie firefighter who was stationed at the door and made his way upstairs. The fire was eerily similar to Elke's. The black burned-out circle sat exactly in front of the master bedroom's door. Again, the light was melted and it pointed like a finger to an ignition point. The only difference was that Brittany's upper floor was larger, with more places for an arsonist to hide.

He took a photo.

The man must have been trying to draw attention to Brittany's bedroom, just as he'd tried with Elke's. What about this room in particular was upsetting the arsonist? Had something happened in both of the women's bedrooms? Or did the arsonist randomly pick his victims?

He started to build a profile of the perp. Perhaps he was a man who felt inadequate in his sexual abilities. Maybe he'd been sexually abused as a child. Maybe he had been picked on as a child or rebuked by women as an adult. Therefore, in order for him to find fulfillment, he found a way he could control women and punish them for the mistakes made by the women of his past.

Kevin shrugged. Sounded logical, but he wasn't a professional profiler.

There was a ring of white powder around the scorched carpet, and he took another picture and a sample. Like before, it had a faint scent of chlorine. This time, however, there was a liquid, an oily substance staining the carpet outside of the powder. Grabbing a swab, he took a sample. The liquid was clear and had a distinct petroleum-based scent.

He'd smelled the odor before. He wafted the swab under his nose. He couldn't put his finger on that scent.

He stared at the white powder. Smelled like chlorine. Probably a pool shock treatment. It was easily attainable. Hell, Brittany even had a pool in the backyard. She would likely have something like that on hand.

Chlorine was a hell of an oxidizer. All that had to be added was brake fluid—

Brake fluid.

Why hadn't he figured it out before? It was so easy. Heather and Brittany had both said they witnessed a white smoke and then combustion. It made perfect sense. When the chlorinated isocyanurates from the shock treatment reacted with the ester in the brake fluid, it generated heat, causing the hot liquids in the fluid to give off a mist, and as the heat increased, flame to erupt.

He'd seen these types of fires in several of his practice burns.

Finally he could figure this out. He had the modus operandi narrowed down. The man entered women's homes when only the women were at home and waited for the right moment, when they were asleep or preoccupied, to start the fires. Given that this time there were two women in the house, Kevin had a feeling the perp was growing less afraid of being caught.

The signature of his crime, the way his actions reflected his needs and his personality, was coming to light. This was a man who thought he was above the law. He wanted to watch. He took joy from controlling and dominating women.

The fires weren't an act of rage. They were well planned, well executed and extremely ballsy.

Kevin imagined the man standing where he stood now, in Brittany's master bedroom, calmly waiting, listening to the women talk. Maybe he even took some kind of sexual pleasure in it.

Kevin had the source and a growing profile of the man responsible. He just needed to get his suspect.

On Brittany's dresser was a picture of her and Heather. They were holding wineglasses and pink streamers were strewn around behind them. Heather's hair was longer and she wore a bright blue shirt that made her eyes stand out, but the most beautiful thing about the photo was the smile on her face. Even though it was only a picture, he could sense her joy.

Ever since he'd moved to the neighborhood, he'd noticed Heather. She would always smile and wave and act happy and nice when he'd spoken to her, but it wasn't until last night, when he kissed her, that she'd really seemed to come to life. When she had looked at him, he'd seen that woman, the happy woman in the photograph. It was as though she had forgotten herself and her burden while she was in his arms.

He would do anything to have her look at him like that again. To see the sparkle in her eyes, the heat of her fingers as they rolled his shirt into a ball and she pulled him closer, hungry for more. Something had happened in those precious seconds, something irreversible. At least for him.

Until last night, he hadn't realized how lonely he had become. How badly he wanted a woman. Not just any woman. He wanted Heather.

He picked up the picture and, for a moment, thought about putting it in his pocket. If he hadn't been standing in the middle of a crime scene he would have taken it.

He sat the picture back. Heather was another man's wife; not even a picture of her could belong to him.

On the other hand, he could be a friend. After they had spoken, it had been easy to see that she needed, more than anything else, someone she could trust. Hopefully she would take him up on his offer of staying at his house. Sure, it would be odd at first after what had transpired, but they were both adults. Last night had been nothing more than too much alcohol and too little self-control. They could just slip back into their roles as friends. No big deal.

He would just have to ignore the way she walked... and the way her hair always smelled like flowers...and the way she always said her *R*'s as if they deserved an entire syllable just to themselves. He loved that about her.

Then again, there were so many other things that he loved about her. She was so selfless. She always seemed to care about others more than herself. She had taken such good care of the kids—especially Lindsay. She had been like a mother to her. He could do most things, but Lindsay had needed the guidance of a woman. Lindsay would need even more in the years to come and, without a doubt, Heather could be the woman to give it.

That was, unless he screwed it up. Or if she had to leave town after her divorce.

He couldn't bear the idea of her a thousand miles away, leading a life separate from him. Lindsay would be equally as heartbroken. And Colter, though he may not always have shown it, especially in the past few months, loved Heather, as well. In Colter's world, baseball came first and Heather had always made a point of coming to every game. Sometimes, when she could, she had brought Lindsay down after school and they had sat through the practices. Whenever she sat in the bleachers Colter lit up, his face glowing with pride.

Kevin had depended on Heather so much. Throughout the years she had always been there when he needed an extra hand. After Allison's death, she had taken Lindsay at least once a week. He hadn't realized until now what a huge role she had played in their lives.

But now was not the time to dwell on these thoughts. He had a job to do. He turned back to the task at hand, trying to focus.

Brittany and Nathan's king-size bed was covered in a faux leopard-print fur, complete with pink sheets. There were two walk-in closets, and he entered one. Clearly Brittany's, it was full of shiny clothes and accessories, and one entire wall was covered in shoes of every color.

Nathan's closet was only half-full, but everything was meticulously hung on wooden hangers. His shirts, pants, jackets and belts were kept separate and then further organized according to color. On the floor beneath the clothes was a line of shoes, just as carefully arranged. At the end of the closet, in the far corner, sat a pair of boots. They lay on the floor askew, as if someone had taken them off and thrown them in. They looked out of place in the meticulous order of Nathan's closet.

He took a picture and then carefully lifted the left boot. The toe of the boot had a faint white residue on its tip and he took a sample. The sole was covered in stars, the outside edge sported rectangular squares. And it was a size ten. Kevin scrolled back in his camera, searching for his picture of the print he'd taken in Elke's garage. When he found it, his pulse jumped.

He had his match.

He studied the boot further. It had been well-worn, the star and rectangular edging worn thin near the big toe and the heel, and the sole had been forced flat, the rubber permanently squished out of the sides. Whoever had worn these had been a heavy man, heavier than Nathan Miller.

He turned back to the closet and picked up one of Nathan's shoes. Size twelve. Either Nathan's feet had shrunk or the boots belonged to someone else, someone who hoped to hide evidence in plain sight.

The brand was one Kevin recognized from the local chain department store where thousands of the same type of boots had likely been sold over the past few years. There would be no way he could trace sales back concisely enough to be of any use. Yet the owner must have been the type to be on a budget. These weren't the expensive boots worn by loggers as Tracy, Elke's neighbor, had assumed. They were cheaper, more common, though they did match her description.

He carefully slipped the boots into an evidence bag and set it in his duffel.

It was strange, the one solid lead he had on his suspect had been discarded on the scene. Why? Why hadn't the boot's owner kept them? Thrown them in some random Dumpster where they would have never been found? Was the arsonist purposely leaving clues behind, leading Kevin on a trail of breadcrumbs? Or was he confident he would never be caught?

The thought pissed Kevin off, but he tried to keep his emotions in check. He didn't have time to be angry.

He glanced down at his notebook. His notes were finally starting to take shape:

Dark-haired man
Average build
Midforties
Sets fires outside of master bedroom doors
Chlorine/brake fluid fires
Heavier man
Size 10 boot
Likes to control
May watch the fires
Enjoys reaction

There was one note that still bothered him and, as he stared at it, it seemed to fade and sharpen like a blinking neon sign.

Motive?

He had no idea how the two victims were connected. Elke was in an entirely different socio-economic bracket, different education background, single and, though Elke was pretty in an average way, she couldn't compete with Brittany's appeal.

It seemed unlikely that whoever was behind this was sleeping with both women, but he could be wrong. Maybe the women had upset the suspect in some way while they were having an affair. Or maybe it had nothing to do with their bedroom behavior, and the fact that the suspect set the fires outside their doors had something more to do with mommy issues.

He had so many questions and so few answers.

Patience. Study. Evaluation.

He would get his answers.

He made his way downstairs. The carpet squelched as he walked through the area. The walls were blackened, the paint was scorched and blistered, and the air smelled of acrid, chemically laced smoke.

He made his way into the garage, hoping there would be another clue. Brittany's car was in the garage, the keys hanging loosely on a rack. Nathan's keys and truck were gone, substantiating Brittany's claim of his being at the local country club at the time of the fire. He'd still need to talk to the club to verify his alibi, but he doubted Nathan had any part in the fire.

There was no clear point of entry. All the windows in the house were intact. It was hard to say how long the suspect had been waiting in the house but, according to Heather, she'd been in the home for at least thirty minutes and had heard no one come in. Yet at some point the suspect had entered the house and made his way upstairs. It must have been before Heather's arrival and after Nathan had unlocked the door when he'd left. Perhaps when Brittany had been in her room to get dressed after Nathan had left. Which meant the perpetrator must have been in the house for almost an hour.

Why had he waited to start the fire? He couldn't have known Heather was on her way over unless he was close to Heather or he'd heard Brittany inviting her.

If he had heard Brittany's invitation and chose to wait, did that mean the suspect knew Heather? Or was there another reason? Did he want to send a message to both women?

Kevin took his time as he looked around the yard. There was nothing out of place in the front, so he made his way around back to the pool's shed. The doors were locked so he peered in through the window. In the darkness, he could make out the rows of well-organized supplies, brushes and hoses. Everything seemed in order and undisturbed.

He made a note: "Suspect likely supplied powder. None stolen from Brittany's pool supply."

A long row of bushes ran along the side of the garage and under the house's back windows. In a bush beneath the back window, something white caught his eye. Putting on his gloves, Kevin took a picture and then picked up the object. It was a long white bottle with a red-and-blue label. Brake fluid from Truck Boys, a local auto parts store.

He carefully slid the bottle into an evidence bag. Perhaps the lab could pull prints. Then again, asking them for another test meant more money.

At least he finally had concrete evidence—evidence that backed his hypothesis on the ignition source.

Yet, assuming this bottle had held the fluid used to ignite the fire, why was it in the backyard? This was where Heather had seen the man standing. Was it possible he had dropped it by accident, or had he intentionally planted another clue?

Kevin would be a fool to underestimate his suspect.

There was nothing in the grass or dirt near the bottle, nothing to give away the suspect's intention.

He looked up, through the window. The front door was directly in view. A chill ran down his spine. The man had watched as Heather and Brittany had rushed to the door, watched as they must have questioned what had happened.

He must have wanted to see the results of his work; that was, until he'd seen Heather looking at him.

His crimes weren't going to stop, but God only knew what direction his next crime would take. A man like this, a man who got excited watching the fear and pain of others, was dangerous. If he thought Heather could identify him, that put her directly in danger.

It was hard to say what this perp was capable of. All Kevin could do was set a trap the egomaniacal suspect couldn't resist.

He called Detective Lawrence.

"We just had another fire. I'm sure it was started by the same man from the other night, but I haven't got a handle on who he is yet."

"So what do you want me to do?"

"I want you to call a press conference. We need to pull this guy out into the public eye."

Chapter Thirteen

Heather stood in the bank teller's line. Her stomach ached as she anticipated what she might find. She kept her eyes on the man who waited in line in front of her. The way he wrung his hands and stepped from one foot to the other made Heather think of David. If he'd come in, would he have had the same washed-out pallor, sweaty brow and squashed facial expression?

She doubted it. David wasn't the type. He was the kind of man who would step up to the Devil with a haughty grin. If he made his way through these doors, he'd probably saunter to the desk and charm the teller while he stripped their accounts bare. He'd probably even get her phone number on his way out the door.

"Ma'am?" one of the tellers called from behind her. "May I help you?"

Heather stood there a moment. If she found out David had not touched their accounts, she would feel crazy. Her suspicion would only validate David's opinion that she was the problem. Yet, if she didn't check her accounts, Kevin would think her a fool.

She had learned enough in the past few days to know she couldn't trust David to be fair or just. He could only be trusted to do the wrong or hurtful thing. She needed to protect herself. She needed to be strong and safeguard herself.

Her hands shook violently as she turned and made her way to the counter. "I need to check my accounts." She handed the teller the slip where she'd written her account numbers. "Could you print out the balances?"

"No problem," the woman said, tapping away on her keyboard.

As she waited, her heart beat so loudly she was almost positive the teller could hear it.

"Okay," the teller said, her face pinched slightly as she held out a printout.

Heather took it and looked down at the paper that would tell her her future.

Account Summary
Savings Balance…$150
Checking Balance…$50

Heather sucked in a breath. Her head swam in a chilling fog.

He had done it.

He had cleared their accounts.

She had nothing.

"Can you print me out a record of all account activity for the past six months?" Heather asked, her voice barely making ripples in her trance.

The woman nodded. "Are you okay, Mrs. Sampson?"

She nodded, afraid that if she spoke tears would start to flow.

The woman tapped another button and handed her a small packet of papers. "Is there anything else that you need, Mrs. Sampson?"

She shook her head, turned away and rushed to her car.

She gripped the printout as if it was the edge of a cliff, and it crinkled in her hand. The world was giving way under her feet as she collapsed into the driver's seat, letting her pounding head rest against the steering wheel.

He'd screwed her. Again.

She had proof. Proof that he cared nothing for her. He didn't care whether she had nothing. He had made a point of keeping her from her life, telling her that college was for "other women" and not her. He had wanted her to concentrate on starting a family. If things were different, she could have been a nurse by now—she could have had everything she needed to start a life on her own. Instead, she had nothing, only the wreckage she had allowed him to create.

She hated him for what he'd done to her and the agony he was inflicting.

Unable to be held back any longer, tears poured from her eyes, coming so fast they splashed into her lap.

Let them pour. Let them rain down and purge her of the pain and shame she felt. Maybe if she cried long enough and hard enough, she would shrivel up and collapse in on herself like a spent balloon. David would be happy to see her gone. His life would be so much easier.

Maybe that could be her last gift to him—to disappear.

She envisioned his life with her dead. He would collect her life insurance. Then, he would find another woman. Take her on vacation on the profits of Heather's death. They would drink. Make love. Tell each other their passions. He would tell her the tales of his childhood. He'd tell her secrets he'd once whispered in Heather's ear after a long night of making love until their bodies ached and their sheets were dewy with sweat.

Rivers of tears sluiced down her cheeks, contorting her face in the rearview mirror. It was the perfect picture, her face ripped apart by pain. David would have loved to see her now. The mess he'd created.

He had played God with her, just like he did with everyone else.

She couldn't let him do this. She couldn't let him play God anymore. He needed to be stopped and she was the one to do it. She had nothing left to lose.

Wiping the tears from her face, she dialed her lawyer.

"Have you had a chance to look over my prenuptial agreement, Ms. Kohl?" she asked when the lawyer responded.

"Oh yes, Mrs. Sampson, I was just about to call you."

From the trepidation in Ms. Kohl's voice, Heather doubted what she said was true.

There was a rustle of paperwork before the lawyer continued. "Actually, I did find some things that are rather interesting. However, there are several amendments that may be upsetting."

She had already had enough for one day, but she steeled herself. Once she heard what she had to hear, it would be over.

"What?" Her tone was tight, like a bullwhip cracking in the air.

"First there is a clause that states if either of you is to separate and leave the home for more than seven days, that person will be held liable for all legal costs accrued during the divorce settlement." Ms. Kohl exhaled. "I've been in contact with Dr. Sampson's lawyer, Mr. Deschamps."

Heather cringed at the name. He would have been her first choice if she could have afforded him. The gray-haired lawyer was known statewide for his role in most high-end divorce cases. David was pulling out all the stops to make sure she got nothing.

"Mr. Deschamps said, in no uncertain terms, that Dr. Sampson will not be gone from your residence for longer than that seven day period. In short, Mrs. Sampson, Dr. Sampson will soon be moving back into your home, where he must reside for two uninterrupted weeks before he may leave again. If he doesn't stay for those two weeks, or if he should fail to return to your main residence, he will be responsible for not only his legal costs, but yours, as well."

She let the news sink in. David was going to come home. He wasn't the type to let the knife sit at the surface, he always pressed until he drew blood.

"May I leave?" The thought of living in the same household with David again made the bile rise in her throat.

"You may, but the same rules apply. If I may, Mrs. Sampson, I recommend you stay in your home. Let's keep things as civil and quiet as we can."

"Civil in the sense that we have an amicable divorce? That we don't steal each other's money?" Heather said, her voice coming from somewhere so deep it clawed at her throat.

"Has he done something I need to know about, Mrs. Sampson?"

"He took everything he could from our bank accounts." He'd left only the bare minimums, so that he didn't need her signature to officially close the accounts. "I have no money and no liquid assets." She twisted in her seat at her admission and the fear Ms. Kohl would quit after finding out that, for the moment, she wouldn't be paid.

"I'm new to divorce law, but I've seen this before. For now, send me your financial records and I'll try to prove he is misallocating your marital assets. At the very least, I can get you some funds to help you get back on your feet."

Finally, there was a glimmer of hope in the darkness. She would still be at others' mercy, but now it would only be until she could get her money back.

"Do you think you could get a job, some source of income while I work with Mr. Deschamps in getting some funds returned?"

She thought of Kevin's offer to watch the kids after school. He'd even offered her a room.

"I can."

"Great," Ms. Kohl said. "Now, there's another section here about extramarital affairs and their impact on the validity and terms of your agreement."

A man got into the truck that was parked next to her. He glanced over and looked at her as though he could hear her conversation. Heather couldn't bear the weight of his gaze and she looked away.

"What does that mean, Ms. Kohl?"

"As it reads, if it is proven you have an extra-marital relationship you get nothing, but if your husband has an extramarital affair, your prenup will be null and void."

"Okay." She thought of her kiss with Kevin. His lips had been hard and wanting, searching for more but resistant to taking things toward the bedroom. "What constitutes an extramarital affair?"

There was another rustle of paper as Ms. Kohl must have flipped through the prenup. "There's nothing that clearly defines what actions shall be defined as an extramarital affair, so that could be a way to get the entire prenup dismissed. If we can do that, we have a chance of getting you a fair and equitable division of assets."

"Would a kiss be considered an extramarital affair?" Heather asked, her voice low.

"Is there any evidence of the kiss? Photos? Videos?"

"No. Not that I know of."

"Well, unless there is evidence of Dr. Sampson kissing another woman, then there is little we can do. We need to find either some sort of proof or a credible witness to the event in order to pursue legal action."

Heather's cheeks burned. Ms. Kohl had misunderstood her meaning. She gave a light cough and looked around to make sure no one in the bank's parking lot was paying her any mind. "What if *I* kissed someone?"

"Oh… Well…" Ms. Kohl paused for a moment as she must have collected herself. "It would weaken our case, even though Montana is a no-fault state. I would recommend you don't put yourself in a position that would adversely affect any possible settlements."

If she found herself alone with Kevin again, she couldn't repeat her mistake. She couldn't allow her body to overrule her mind. "Not a problem, Ms. Kohl."

"In the meantime, you may want to start doing a little digging on your husband. You can do this yourself or you can hire a private investigator. If you can, we need to find direct evidence of an affair. That is, if David returns home. For now, the ball is in his court."

As usual David held the power position. At least she had a play. She could go home and get to work on building up her life while trying to analyze the fine details of his.

"Thank you, Ms. Kohl."

"You're very welcome. Please don't hesitate to contact me should you need anything else."

"Thank you."

"And Ms. Sampson?"

"Yes, Ms. Kohl?"

"I look forward to taking your husband down. Have a good afternoon." She hung up, not waiting for Heather's response.

For the first time since she had met her lawyer, she truly liked the woman. Maybe Ms. Kohl's being a new lawyer wasn't such a bad thing. As a newbie, she still had the passion to work hard to bring down her adversary. And she was still building her reputation. If she could win this case against the infamous pit bull, Mr. Deschamps, it could be a strong foundation for her career.

A career. That was something Heather was lacking. Until the two lawyers could come up with some agreement, she needed to come up with some way of making money.

Heather looked down at her phone and scrolled through her contacts. She dialed Kevin.

"Oh, hey, Heather. How did it go at the bank?" he said as soon as he answered.

She swallowed back the lump lodged in her throat. "Not as well as I'd hoped. He took everything."

"Are you okay? Do you need me to do anything?"

God, just hearing his voice made her want to run to

him, but she couldn't. She couldn't risk the damage an affair would cause with her divorce.

"Actually, you can help me."

You could hold me. Tell me everything is going to be okay.

"What do you need?"

"Actually, I was thinking maybe I could take you up on your offer and come to work for you for a while... maybe I could help with the kids?"

She couldn't control the insecurity that welled within her. If she had ever asked David for a job at his office, or in any part of the hospital for that matter, he would have told her to find something else.

"That would be great." Kevin sounded excited. "You'd be saving me. Having you full-time with the kids would really help me out."

She didn't know if she entirely believed him. She had been helping out with his kids for a while, spending an hour here and there after school, but he'd always made things work. Regardless, she was thankful.

"I'll pick the kids up from school today, okay?"

"That would be great," he said. "I have a meeting tonight. I don't know what time I'll be home."

"You want me to keep them at your house?" Heather wasn't sure what David would think, but that didn't matter anymore.

"You're not getting a hotel?"

"I... My lawyer didn't think it was a good idea."

"Oh. Well, I guess at least if you stay at my place for a while, you can make sure the kids get to bed at a reasonable hour." He sounded tired, and maybe a little upset.

After the kids were in bed, she would be nearly

alone, waiting until he came home. Her thighs tingled with unwelcome desire.

"That's fine, but..." She tried to think of something that would keep her heated desire at bay. *David.* Just the thought of having to go home to him turned her emotions cold.

Chapter Fourteen

Kevin stepped out of the crime lab, the evidence bag hanging limp from his shoulder.

He should have been concentrating on what he would say at tonight's meeting, and how he would play his hand; instead, all he could think about was Heather's dark hair. Everything about her seemed fragile, as though, if he reached out too fast or too hard, he risked breaking her or—worse—pushing her away.

There had been something in her voice when she had called, a supplicating tone with an undercurrent of tension, which reminded him of their kiss. The way her lips parted, inviting him to go deeper, to open his heart. Yet their kiss had been flavored with the forbidden.

She deserved someone better than David—someone who would treat her like the beautiful princess she was—even if that man wasn't him.

He imagined her in another man's arms and a strange, unwelcome wave of jealousy coursed through him.

He gripped the strap of his evidence bag so hard that it cut into his hand. He hitched the bag farther up his shoulder. Work needed his attention, not things he couldn't change.

He glanced back at the crime lab where he had dropped off his samples. The techs there had assured him the samples from Elke's house would take a few more days to analyze, and the new set from Brittany's maybe a week. Every moment that slipped by was upping the chances the perpetrator was going to get away. Maybe the fires would stop, maybe the arsonist would get scared after his run-in with Heather, but Kevin doubted he would get that lucky.

The perpetrator was getting bolder, looking in the back window of Brittany's home—and nearly being identified.

A couple walked by Kevin as they made their way out of the crime lab, the man's face pinched and the woman's eyes red. They reminded him of the many victims he had seen during his tenure. He couldn't let another fire happen. He couldn't let someone get hurt.

Kevin walked toward his truck. Detective Lawrence was leaning against the driver's door, his arms were crossed over his chest.

Lawrence used to work for the Drug Task Unit. To most, the man would have been an intimidating presence as he was built like a Mack truck on steroids, his neck disappearing between his boxy head and wide shoulders. To Kevin, he would always be the man whose favorite coffee mug had a picture of Hello Kitty.

Kevin stopped beside him. "Hey, Detective. Did you get the meeting set?"

"Seven o'clock, on the courthouse steps." Lawrence unfolded his arms. "The mayor wants to make a big show of it for the media. By the way, in case you were wondering, your battalion chief is a pain in the ass. He always so helpful?"

Kevin smirked. "Hiller's about as accommodating as a porcupine, but once you get to know him…" He paused as he thought about the BC. "Scratch that. You're right—he's always a pain in the ass."

Lawrence laughed as he pushed off from the truck. "So what do you have on our suspect? Anything I can help you with?"

Kevin pulled out the fire investigation report, the camera and his notebook and laid them on the hood of his truck. "Feel free to take a look."

Lawrence stepped beside him and picked up the fire reports. He studied them for a moment, flipping through the pages.

"Do you think it's possible your perp had been sleeping with both women, or at least been attempting to seduce them?"

Kevin thought of Brittany, her long blond hair draping like a curtain over her face, hiding the secrets in her eyes. She was beautiful and she seemed to have a good relationship with her husband, but that didn't mean that their marriage was perfect or that they didn't have secrets.

"It would be a strong motivator." Kevin leaned against the truck. "But so far this investigation is going nowhere."

"It's fun to be thrown a curveball once in a while, ain't it?" Lawrence said, glancing up. "Keeps us on our toes."

This case was doing that, but rather than being on his toes, Kevin felt more as if he was in a free fall with the ground nowhere in sight.

"I suppose. And hey, I appreciate your taking the time to lend me a hand. It's nice to have another set of eyes on this."

Detective Lawrence waved him off. "Taking bastards down is what keeps me going. We'll just have to make sure the district attorney will want to move on this. Right now, with everything you've shown me, there hasn't been much damage, no loss of life. Even if we file charges, she may decide to pass on this one."

"You think so? Even if this is a serial arsonist?"

"Two doesn't make a serial arsonist. If there were three on the other hand… But it all depends on the DA's mood. You know how it is. Sometimes they're busier than hell, other times what they take on is completely dependent on politics and the budget."

It seemed crazy to him that justice could only come at the price of loss of life or another person's home. Then again, he shouldn't have been surprised. He'd been a firefighter long enough to know that those who deserved to be caught and punished were often the ones who had enough experience with the legal system to know how to evade its grasp.

"This budget crap sounds familiar. Hiller has been on my back with these investigations. I think he shares the DA's opinion of the importance of prosecution. The only thing he's worried about is the department's bottom line."

"At least you have the media on your side. If they weren't covering this, it would've already been swept under the rug."

"I'm hoping it's going to help smoke out our perpetrator."

"What do you make of this guy?"

"He likes the control, the manipulation and the thrill."

"Then your subject will be there tonight." Lawrence nodded. "How do you think we can get an ID on him?"

"We need to bring up the ass-pucker factor. Give him something that only he'll see and realize the true meaning of. Something he won't be able to take his eyes off."

"I like it. You have something in mind?"

"I'm thinking the bottle of brake fluid." He grabbed his camera, flipped through the pictures until he pulled up the photo of the bottle stuffed under the bush. "We should take this picture, blow it up and make sure it gets plastered somewhere at the meeting that's out of the line of sight—somewhere the perp would have to make a special effort to see."

Lawrence took the camera and scanned through the rest of the pictures. He stopped at one of Brittany in her yard. "We should blow this one up, too. Then have the Miller woman come up and talk about her loss. The media will love it. Plus, it'll build the pressure for your department to get a hold on this perp and give you more time. You're going to need it."

"In the meantime, I want to speak to Elke. See if I can dig a little more information out of her. Maybe I can get her to come." He took the camera from Lawrence. "Can you help me get all the pieces in place for the meeting? I'll email you the pictures. Can you get them printed?"

"No problem. Tonight, when we get things rolling, I'll talk for a while. Give you an intro and the mayor a little lip service. While I'm working, you look for your man."

Kevin nodded. "Let's get this bastard."

Chapter Fifteen

Heather sat in her car, waiting for Lindsay in front of the elementary school. Once the bell rang, children poured from the doors. They swarmed toward the parking lot in a wave of dropped papers and swinging backpacks. Near the back, with her pack sagging from her shoulders, was Lindsay.

She waved at the girl, catching her attention, and Lindsay made her way over.

"Am I riding with you today?" Lindsay asked.

"Yep, your dad asked me to pick you and your brother up," Heather said.

Lindsay opened the back door and thumped down in the seat. "We don't have to pick up Colter."

"Why?" Heather checked to make sure Lindsay was buckled in before she merged into the meandering stream of cars leaving the school.

"Colter has a game today."

"I totally forgot."

"It's okay. Dad forgets about the games all the time."

Heather glanced in the mirror at Lindsay. "Do you think that's upsetting Colter?"

"I dunno, but he and Dad have been mad at each

other a lot." Lindsay shrugged. "Does that mean Colter's going to leave?"

"What do you mean, Lindsay?"

"Well," Lindsay said, looking at her. "You know. You and David fight. That's why he left. People fight and then one of them leaves."

"No, Lindsay," Heather said, her heart lurching. "When people love each other, they don't leave just because they fight. Colter and your dad love each other. I promise."

"If Dad loved Colter, he would come to all the games, just like you do."

She had to get Kevin to come. She couldn't stand seeing the disappointment etched in Lindsay's face, disappointment that would be echoed on Colter's face when he realized his father wasn't there.

"Your dad loves you both—there's no doubt in my mind. But I'll talk to your dad about coming to the game. I'm sure he's probably already on his way," she lied.

Lindsay shrugged. "Whatever."

Once Heather was parked in the high school lot, she dialed Kevin, but the call went to voice mail. She left a message, telling him she and Lindsay hoped to see him at the game.

Then she took the girl's hand and went to find a seat on the risers. Her eyes scanned the first players who came out of the locker room. A sensation crept through her, telling her something was wrong when she didn't find Colter among the last players who stepped onto the field.

Heather made her way down the risers and toward the dugout.

Mr. T, his coach, had his back to her. His wide neck had been sunburned early on in the season, but now, after a month in the sun, it had taken on a nice toasted caramel color.

"Coach T?"

He turned slightly, like moving his entire frame was too much of an effort. "Mrs. Sampson. What can I do for you?"

She stepped closer. "Hey, Coach, I was just noticing Colter wasn't out of the locker room yet."

Mr. T frowned. "He's not *in* the locker room. I took him out of today's game. He's been missing too many practices."

"What?"

The coach must have had it wrong. Colter wasn't the type to miss baseball. It was his life. So much so that she wouldn't have been surprised if Colter slept with his mitt tucked under his pillow.

"I sent a note home." He stabbed his toe into the dirt.

"But, Coach—" she started to argue, but he cut her off with a wave of his hand.

"Hated doing it. But he was a bad example for the younger players. They need to see that just because you're a top player doesn't mean you can cut practice and expect to play—even during semifinals."

She could understand, but this wasn't like Colter. He wasn't cocky and caught up in all the trappings that came with being a star athlete. He was better than that. He'd always kept his humility.

"I'm sure he isn't cutting practice because he thinks he's some hotshot. He…he isn't that kind of kid. I know him. I swear."

Mr. T nodded, but he stared at the dirt. "I wouldn't

have thought so either, but lately there's been something going on with him. Hasn't been acting right. Tried to talk to him. Didn't get much. Just said he was busy."

Busy? For his entire life Colter had only been busy with two things—baseball and homework.

"I'll talk to Colter. Good luck with your game."

"Let him know I'm looking forward to getting him back, but he needs to show me he's serious. I know there're a few college scouts that have got their eyes on him."

She nodded. Colter had been talking about going to Washington for baseball since he first started playing. That had been his dream. Whatever was going on must have been major if he'd let it hold him back, but what could it possibly be?

"I'll let him know." She tried to smile, but her lips barely registered her attempt. Between her life's upheavals, Brittany's and now Colter's it didn't feel right to even try to fake happiness.

She made her way back to the stands where Lindsay looked up from the book that had kept her busy when Heather was gone.

"What's the matter?" the girl asked.

"Nothing, sweetheart, everything's okay."

Maybe she couldn't control the storm in her own life, but she vowed to be there for Colter, Lindsay and Kevin. They needed her.

THE FRONT DOOR of Kevin's house was unlocked when they got home, but there was no sign of Colter anywhere, not even in his room, according to Lindsay who'd run to check.

"Is there anywhere else you think he'd go?" Heather asked her, but the girl only shook her head.

"I'm going to run to my house and give your dad a call. Will you be okay for a few?" From there, she could talk to Kevin openly.

"I'll be fine," Lindsay said.

Heather walked to the front door just as Lindsay clicked on the television and the sound of children's voices filled the empty house.

She made her way to her house. In the middle of the living room was David. His scrub bottoms were heaped in a pile by the foot of the couch and his top was thrown over the table next to the door. He sat on the couch wearing only his black skintight boxer briefs. He looked up at her with shock on his face.

"I thought you were at the baseball game. It's Friday." His look of surprise was quickly replaced by anger.

She didn't know what to say or do. The last thing she had expected was to find David nearly naked on the couch.

She couldn't stand looking at his sweaty, personal-trainer sculpted chest, and she quickly looked away. "I needed something."

"Now isn't a good time, Heather." He looked toward the steps leading upstairs.

"This isn't a good time? You may have been forced to move back in, but this is my house."

"How dare you talk to me like that?" David said as he stood up and slipped on his scrub pants. "I paid for this damn place. Without me, you'd have nothing."

"Stop it, David," she whispered.

"What did you just say to me?" He stormed toward

her, his face so close she could see the sweat oozing from each pore on his nose.

She stood still, afraid that if she dared to move a muscle, David would lose control. "I said…" She spoke slowly, the words curdling in her fear.

"What?" He grabbed hold of her arms and squeezed her. "Just like I thought. Nothing. There's nothing in your damn head."

She stepped back, out of his grasp, and out of the anger-laced scent of his hot breath. "Aren't you supposed to be at work? And why are you half-naked?"

"I took the day off." He turned away from her and grabbed his shirt, slipping it back on. "I'm moving back in."

"I know." Trepidation churned in her belly. She didn't want to share this house with him. The truth hit hard. She wanted to be in Kevin's house, with him. Kevin would never treat her the way David had. Instead, he would worship her, just as he had when he'd kissed her.

She recalled that moment in his arms, his lips against hers… When he had pulled away, it hadn't been to shame her, it had been to save her from regret. In that moment, he had saved her in the only way he could. And now, when she needed even more help, he was there for her again, offering her a job, a safe place to stay and a distraction from the agony of her life.

She would give anything to be with a man who would raise her up instead of break her down. For so long, she hadn't realized how badly David treated her, how wrong it was when he grabbed her beneath the arm, pinching her until her flesh bruised. She had blindly loved him. She had forgiven him his trespasses. She had taken the blame and accepted fault for his actions.

Every time he'd lost his temper or raged, she had accepted responsibility—if she just hadn't said what she said, or worn what she'd worn, he would never have lost control. She was living the cycle of abuse and now was her chance to start to break free.

David looked at her, his icy gaze filled with contempt.

"If you're going to stay here, I'm not," she said. "At least not until I have to, as the prenuptial agreement stipulates. For the next few days, David, the house is yours."

David's jaw went slack. "What?" He looked at her with confusion.

She turned away from him and made her way upstairs. Grabbing her suitcase, she threw it on the bed and started packing. Now was the time to rekindle her dreams, remember who she was and stop living a life that was no longer her own.

Chapter Sixteen

Kevin pulled up to Elke Goldstein's house. He'd tried to call her, but there had been no answer and, once again, he found himself running after shadows.

The windows were open, probably in her attempt to rid the scent of smoke from her house until she could get the money from her insurance company to pay for a restoration company. The neighbor Mrs. Jones and her son were out in the front yard watering the garden, and she waved as he made his way to Elke's front door.

"She's not home," Mrs. Jones yelled.

"You know where she went?"

"Some guy in a white car came to pick her up a few hours ago." She stopped watering for a moment. "She didn't say where she was going, but I've seen the car there before… In fact, I think the guy driving it was the guy she had over the night of the fire."

Elke had told him she hadn't seen or heard from the man since the day of the fire and that she didn't have his phone number. Now, all of sudden, they were meeting? He had told her to contact him if she heard from the man again. His hackles rose. Elke knew more than what she had told him, but why had she kept the truth from him?

Kevin made his way down the steps and toward Mrs. Jones. "Do you know the model of the car?"

"Well, it was white. Small." She shook her head. "My husband is the one who knows cars."

"That's fine, no worries. Can you tell me if the car was a sports car or a sedan?"

She looked back toward him. "Sports car. Pretty flashy. You don't see them a lot."

Kevin's mind went to David and his white Porsche Carrera. There was only one like it in Missoula. He shook off the thought. Just because someone he knew drove a car that somewhat resembled the one described didn't mean David was his man.

Then again…

"Was the car a Porsche by chance? Has an emblem on the hood that's yellow, red and black with a horse."

"Yep." Mrs. Jones smiled with relief. "That's it. Looks like a family crest kind of shape." She made the shape with her fingers.

Elke had admitted the man was her lover, which meant David was cheating on Heather.

His anger flared, but he tamped down his emotions as he struggled to remain logical. Now wasn't the time to let his emotions cloud his judgment. It never ended well.

For a moment, he was back at the last fire he'd fought three years ago. He was standing in the doorway of the burning house, tongues of fire licking the walls around him as he made his way inside. A child had been on the second floor, an eight-year-old girl, and her screams were nearly drowned out by the whipping crackle and roar of the beast.

Many nights he'd heard that voice in his dreams. He'd awaken to the smell of smoke, a scent that had invaded his dreams and spilled out into his reality. He'd run down the hall to Lindsay's or Colter's room, only to remember that the smell and the sounds were nothing more than a dream.

That was the moment he'd lost his edge.

He couldn't let that happen again.

Just because David had been with Elke didn't mean he was having an affair, and just because David was at the scene didn't mean he had started the blaze. It just meant maybe he knew something, something he had been trying to keep hidden. Or maybe the man Mrs. Jones had seen wasn't David at all, maybe she was just mistaken. Elke had made a point of telling him the man who'd been to her house had been named Anthony, not David.

There were so many possibilities. He just needed to follow the leads and hope that he could find his arsonist and stop the fires. But what if the investigation led him straight to David? What if David *was* the one responsible?

In many ways, David fit the profile. He liked to be in control and dominate women. Liked to play God. Thought he was above the law. The fires had been thought out and extremely ballsy. The only thing that didn't fit the profile was the fact David wasn't sexually inadequate—he didn't fit the bill as a man who was regularly turned down by women. David was confident and, from the way he'd soaked in Brittany's attentions at the barbecue, easygoing when it came to women. Well, all women except his wife.

He treated Heather as though she was a possession he owned and could use as he wanted, or throw away when he found something better.

No matter how much Kevin despised the man, it

didn't make him the arsonist. With Mrs. Jones's sighting, it made him a suspect. And Kevin's only solid lead.

He turned to Mrs. Jones. "Thanks for your help. If you see anything else, please let me know. I appreciate your cooperation."

Kevin rushed back to his truck. He would need to talk to David to find out exactly why he had been going to Elke's house and to see if he could find something that would tie David to the fire at Brittany's. If everything went well, he could nail David.

He got into his truck and dialed Elke. No answer.

He looked down at his screen as a voice mail popped up from Heather.

Had she found out something about David?

He went to his voice mail and was met with Heather's voice. She sounded somewhat frantic as she reminded him about Colter's game.

Damn it. Not again.

He was so sick of failing his son. Erasing the message, he threw his phone on top of his dashboard, pushing the envelope from Colter's coach into view.

He picked up the envelope and ripped it open. Each word seared into him.

Dear Mr. Jensen,
I'm writing to let you know that due to Colter's recent uptick in absences, his dropping GPA (the only class he's currently not at risk of failing is auto shop) and his overall disregard for authority, I have made the decision to bench him...

The letter continued, but Kevin stopped reading. He glanced at the clock. He had three hours before tonight's meeting. Between now and then, he needed to question David and talk to Colter about what was going on.

If he went to see David first, he would be failing his son again.

He was tired of getting pulled in a thousand directions. Tired of always making the right choice for one, but the wrong choice for another. Well, this time, he was going to do what was right for his family. His son needed him.

He turned the truck around as he dialed Colter.

"Hello?" Colter answered, sounding annoyed. "Why is everyone calling?"

"Because everyone's worried. I just got a letter from your coach. You want to talk to me about it? What's going on with you, Colter?"

"Damn it, Dad. I don't have time for this."

"Really? I would think that if you aren't at baseball and you're failing your classes that you would have plenty of time." The moment the words passed his lips he wished he could take them back. He'd get nowhere if he was confrontational.

"I have to go, Dad. I have crap to do."

He tried to control his anger. "What are you doing?"

"I—" Colter paused. "I'm studying. I have a Spanish test tomorrow."

He wanted to believe him even though every bit of him thought Colter was lying. "Really?"

"Look, Dad, it's not like I wanted to be taken out of the game. I just have to deal with some stuff and then everything'll be fine. Now, I have to go study. Okay?"

"Okay, but be home before five. I'm not done talking with you. We need to figure some things out, bud."

"Fine."

The line went dead.

Heather's car was parked in front of his house when Kevin got home. Lindsay was sitting on the front porch with a book in her hands and she looked up as he approached. Her eyes were full of storm clouds.

He knelt beside her, taking her hand in his. "You okay, sweetheart?"

"Yeah, Daddy." She smiled, but the movement of her lips didn't match the look in her eyes. "Colter isn't here. Mrs. Sampson's worried. I shouldn't have told her that he wasn't in his room."

"Sweetheart, it's not *your* fault."

Lindsay nodded, but her gaze moved to the ground. "But, Daddy, I got Colter in trouble. He's gonna be so mad at me."

"You didn't get him in trouble. Colter got himself in this mess. He's not mad at you."

"Yes, he is. The other day I walked into his room without knocking. He screamed at me, Daddy."

He smiled as he thought of all the reasons a teenage boy would be angry at his sister for barging into his room. "Don't worry. But maybe next time knock. It's no big deal. Really. He loves you."

"That's not what he said. He said he wished that I was never born."

That didn't sound like Colter. Ever since Lindsay had been born, he had doted on his baby sister, and when Allison had died, Colter had picked up where she had left off, taking on a role of the other parent and helping to raise his sister.

Maybe that was where everything had started to go wrong. Maybe Kevin should never have let his son take on so much responsibility. Maybe he should have just let him be a kid.

Kevin squeezed Lindsay's hand. "I'm sorry. I'm sure Colter didn't mean what he said. I'll make sure that he talks to you. Okay?"

Lindsay nodded, but he could feel from the way her little hand tensed that she didn't really believe him. Would a mother have handled the situation better? What would Allison have done?

It had been so long since she'd left him that he could just barely remember her face, or the sound of her voice, but he knew she would have done the right thing, something that would have ended with a hug and Lindsay smiling.

No matter how many years passed or how much experience he had, he always felt inadequate as a father. Would it ever change?

"Is Heather still here?" he asked.

"No." Lindsay shook her head. "She had to run back to her house. She's been gone for a while."

He looked over to Heather and David's white house. The lights were on in the living room and David's Porsche was in the driveway.

He gritted his teeth. David had better not have touched her.

"Why don't you go inside, Lindsay?" He helped her stand up and wrapped his arms around her, pulling her into his chest. "I love you, baby girl." He let go of her and lifted her chin so he could look into her eyes. "No matter what happens, that will never change. Everything's going to get better. Trust me."

Lindsay smiled. "I love you, too, Daddy."

It was amazing how fast a few sweet words could mend the spirit.

"I'll be right back."

She walked to the door and twisted the handle. "Okay, Daddy."

He went to his truck and took out his notepad and investigation report and then turned to the Sampson house. The television's blue light flickered in the windows. As he made his way across the yard, he felt like a dead man walking.

Logic. Logic had to be his plan. He couldn't go in there and let David see how he was really feeling. And he certainly couldn't go in there and punch the bastard in the throat like he wanted to.

He rapped on the door, the hollow sound reverberating in the empty street.

"Heather, answer the door!" David yelled from somewhere inside the house.

She didn't answer, but at least she was there.

"Damn woman," David growled as his footsteps moved toward the door. It opened with a creak. His frown tightened. "What're you doing here? Didn't get enough of my wife the other night?"

"What are you talking about?" Kevin took a step back, but forced himself to stop retreating.

"I caught her doing her walk of shame. She tried to lie to me. To tell me nothing happened between you two, but she's always been a terrible liar."

His fists tightened at his sides, but he didn't move. "Nothing happened, David." The man's name felt like ash in his mouth. "Heather's just a friend. Nothing more."

His thoughts flashed to her lips pressed against his, the sweet flavor of her kiss and the heat of her body.

"You're just as bad a liar as she is, Kev. The good news for you is that I don't care. Not about her and definitely not about you or what you do to her. She's not my problem anymore."

"Funny you should talk to me about lying, *Dave*. Where were you last Wednesday night?" He opened his notebook.

"Why do you care?" David leaned against the door. "Need to know my schedule so you can have more time with my wife?"

Kevin reached into his back pocket and pulled out his wallet. He opened it to the badge he kept for moments like these. "Dr. Sampson, my name is Kevin Jensen, I'm the Missoula City fire inspector and I'm here to ask you a few questions."

"Are you kidding me? You're really going to pull the *inspector* crap with me?" David laughed. "Well, I haven't done anything and I don't have any information to give you."

"I'll be the judge of that. You just need to answer a few questions."

"What right do you have to ask me anything?"

"Dr. Sampson, you can answer my questions willingly or I can have a detective show up to your door and take you into custody. Right now, we have reason to believe you are a suspect in an arson."

David's face drained of its color and his eyes shifted to the left. "I've done nothing."

Kevin closed his wallet and slipped it back into his pocket. Maybe Kevin couldn't punch him in the throat, but he could still make him suffer. "If you answer my questions willingly and to the best of your knowledge,

I will make sure to note your cooperation in my investigation report."

David's gaze fell to the notepad in Kevin's hands. "I don't know what you're talking about."

"Let's start again. Where were you on Wednesday night at about 8:00 p.m.?"

David stepped back, recoiling from the question. He looked back over his shoulder as if he was looking for a place to run, but there was no running. There was no hiding. There were only questions and answers.

"Like I said, Dr. Sampson, if you choose, I can have you taken into custody. Knowing you and your reputation as an upstanding doctor within the community, I'm sure this would be the last thing you'd want anyone to know about."

David turned back and faced him. His eyes were dark, like two black holes absorbing all the energy and matter that sank into them. Kevin looked away, an illogical part of him fearing that if he looked too long, those gluttonous holes would consume him.

"Wednesday... I had a full schedule of fresh caths that day and my rounds."

"What time did you leave the hospital for the day?"

"I don't know. Maybe five." David continued to lean against the door frame, but his body stiffened, almost defensive.

"Then where did you go?"

David opened his mouth to speak then shut it and gave an exasperated sigh. "I'm sure Heather told you I asked for a divorce. Is that why you're doing this? To act like her knight in shining armor? Think you can help her by coming after me?"

"I assure you, Dr. Sampson, my actions have nothing to do with my personal life. I have a job to do, and right now that job involves questioning you."

David grumbled.

"Now, if you had left Heather, I assume that means you didn't come home after work on Wednesday night?"

"I went to dinner. There's a place not far from the hospital. I go there all the time."

"What restaurant was it?" Kevin pressed.

"Er..." David looked away. "Ruby's."

"Do you remember the name of your waitress?" Kevin quelled his excitement at taking one leap forward in his investigation.

"I think her name was Deer or something."

"Elke?"

"Sure." David glared at him and he shifted his body as if he was a snake trying to slither from danger.

"Where did you go after leaving the diner?"

"I—" David stopped and pushed himself away from the door frame. "Look, do I need to have a lawyer present?"

"Right now, Dr. Sampson, you are not under arrest. I'm merely asking you some questions to help further my investigation. Should you be arrested, you can obtain a lawyer at that time. But if you have not taken an active role in any arson, you should have nothing to worry about."

Sometimes he loved amping up the ass-pucker factor and making someone step into a box that they themselves had built.

"Well, like I said, I didn't *do* anything."

"Then this little tête-à-tête shouldn't be problem." Kevin made some notes in an attempt to increase the pressure. "So what time did you leave Ruby's and where did you go?"

"I guess it was about seven."

"And?"

David stepped outside and closed the front door behind him. "If I tell you the truth, it would be confidential. Wouldn't it?"

"What you tell me is confidential, unless there is a reason for further law enforcement to become involved."

"You won't tell Heather anything?"

His stomach clenched. He needed to be a man who could be trusted to do the right thing, even if that meant withholding something from the woman he cared about.

"Dr. Sampson, it is my hope that nothing you tell me will put either you or me in a compromising position."

David stared at him, crossing his arms over his chest. Kevin had seen a hundred men do the same thing when they were about to admit guilt. The simple action of crossing their arms was instinctual, a primordial urge to protect the core.

He didn't need to ask the question to know the answer, but he had to hear David answer it. "Where did you go when you left the diner?"

"Elke and I went back to her place."

"And?"

"We played Twister. Come on. Do you need me to spell it out for you?"

He could never tell Heather. Unlike David, she couldn't just cross her arms and protect her heart. No. Her heart was already broken—he'd seen it in her eyes, felt it in the way her lips searched his. David's infidelity would only make it worse. He couldn't even stand the thought of inflicting more pain.

David's secret was a weight he could shoulder, a weight he could keep from bearing down on her.

"So you had sex with Elke. What time did you leave?"

"I don't know. It had to be about 2:00 a.m."

"You played Twister for six hours?"

David's lips turned up into a smirk. "What can I say?" He shrugged.

"You can't expect me to believe it went on for six hours."

David laughed. "No, we watched a movie first. Some stupid romantic comedy." He shrugged. "I turned in my man card for a few hours but it got me laid. I guess it worked out."

For a moment, he imagined holding Heather in his arms, her body resting against his as they watched a movie. It was such a simple thing, those minutes spent together, not speaking, just enjoying the story before them. Those moments were something he could only wish for.

He stared at David and, for the first time, he really noticed the fine lines around David's eyes and the wrinkles on his brow.

Kevin could never understand how Heather fell in love with him—then again, most of the time David hid his real self behind a line of crap a mile wide. When he'd first met the man, Kevin had thought he was all right, even kind of funny. There was no going back to that; he'd seen the monster behind the lab coat.

"Did you return to your house at any point after you left at 2:00 a.m. on Wednesday?"

"I stopped by to pick Heather up for Brittany's barbecue and then I dropped her off. After that I left and got a hotel room. Haven't been back to my house until…"

"Until today?" Kevin tapped his pen on his notebook.

David jerked. "Yeah, until today." His body tightened and his jaw clenched.

"Why did you tell Ms. Goldstein your name was Anthony?"

He answered with a tight laugh. "Look, I thought I would have a little fun. There's no harm in that, right?" He looked at Kevin and seemed to mentally backpedal. "I only gave her a fake name because I never thought I'd see her again."

"But you did. Why did you go to see Elke again today?"

"I heard about the fire and I thought I'd talk to her. Set her straight. Tell her the truth about who I was. I didn't do anything. I thought I could make her feel better."

It struck Kevin as funny that this man, who cared nothing about the woman he'd married, seemed to care more about a woman he'd met in a diner. Just when he thought he couldn't like David any less, David surprised him.

"Where's Elke now?"

"I got her a hotel room near mine," David said. "Her house hasn't been fixed up yet. I thought it was the least I could do."

Kevin jabbed his pen into the paper as he thought about how David had emptied his bank accounts so Heather couldn't have access to any funds, only to, a few hours later, spend money on a hotel room for his mistress.

"Is there anyone who can vouch that you left Elke's house at 2:00 a.m. Wednesday morning?"

"Sure. Call anyone working in the Heart Center. I was the on-call doctor and was called into work at two-thirty. I had to come in for a fifty-six-year-old woman with a MI, a myocardial infarction. I had her in the Heart Center until about five-thirty."

Kevin flipped back in his notes, where it said the fire had been reported at 5:03 a.m. So, the jerk had an alibi. Of course he would have to verify David's whereabouts, but he had a feeling it would be rock solid. Surely David knew the hospital was under constant video surveillance. No way would he lie about being there.

David was guilty of many things, but no matter how much Kevin wanted to arrest him and send him to prison, David probably wasn't the arsonist he was looking for.

Then again, maybe David was lying. He had one hell of a reputation for it. Plus he had to know that, at the very least, it would take Kevin a few hours to pull enough strings to check his alibi.

Chapter Seventeen

Heather watched from her bedroom window as Kevin walked back across their lawn and toward his house. Just as he was about to make his way through the hedges, he looked back, almost as if he could sense her watching. Catching his gaze, she couldn't help but notice the dark circles under his eyes and the pain in his expression. She tried to wave to him, but he had already turned away. Her heart ached to see his face again, even if it was only a glance.

For a moment, she considered running outside, catching him and asking him exactly what was wrong to see if she could help.

What had David said?

She grabbed her filled suitcase, heavy with the mementos of her past and hopes for the future, and she made her way downstairs.

"What did you do, David?"

"What did *I* do? What in the hell are you talking about, woman?" David growled, slamming the door shut.

"What's the matter with Kevin?"

David laughed, his sound low and menacing. "Of

course that's who you would care about. You don't care about me. You never have and you never will."

"Sorry, David, I'm just following your example. You haven't cared about me in years."

"What is wrong with you, Heather? These past few days, you've been different." He stared at her as though he was trying to find a loose thread in her resolve, one he could pull until she steadily unraveled. Well, he could search all he wanted, but he wouldn't find it. "I know what you did. You've been having an affair with Kevin. You can't deny it. I can see it on you."

She let out a shocked laugh. Who was David to call her out? He'd left her standing on the side of the road. He'd made her feel worthless. He'd called her every name that he thought would degrade her not only as a woman but as a person. And now he was going to chastise her?

No more.

"How *dare* you, David. You have no right to say anything to me. You may have thought I wasn't good enough, but all I've ever tried to do is make you happy." Her hands shook with anger. "The best thing you ever did for me was to empty our bank accounts. If it hadn't been for that, David, I would've kept on being your fool. I would've kept listening to your lies when you didn't come home. I would've believed you when you told me you'd been at work even though I could smell another woman's perfume on your skin."

The hard lines around David's mouth softened and his mouth pulled into an O.

She lifted up the handle on her suitcase and rolled it to the door. "While I'm gone, I want you to move into the guest room. You're no longer welcome in my bedroom or in my bed. This marriage is truly over."

She opened the door and stepped outside.

"Heather, wait!" David's voice was a tone too high. "The second you walk out that door, you're going to have nothing and no one. No one is ever going to love you."

She slammed the door on everything that was David. If he was what love was, she didn't need it.

She wheeled her suitcase down the driveway and toward Kevin's house.

There was no going back.

Excitement raced through her, but fear was close on its heels.

She would have no one, but how would that be different than what her life had been? The nights David had sat down with her for dinner, the mornings they'd been together in bed, he'd not really been there. His mind was always on something else. For the past few years, she had been alone. She just hadn't realized it.

She made her way up Kevin's driveway as his front door opened. The light from his dining room was on behind him, making him look as though he was basked in golden rays.

"Are you okay, Heather?" Kevin asked.

She nodded.

He took her suitcase from her, his warm hand brushing against hers. "I'm glad you're here."

"I can't believe it... I walked out on him." She looked at Kevin, but no matter how hard she tried, he wouldn't meet her gaze. "What did he say to you?"

"Don't worry, everything's okay." He turned away from her and led her inside.

She wanted to stop him, to turn him around and have him face her, to have him tell her why he couldn't look her in the eyes.

Why did David have to ruin everything? Couldn't he just let her have one thing that wasn't going to hell? Everything he had touched in her life, all the way down to her spirit, he had broken.

"Are you sure that it's okay if I stay, Kevin? I can go. I'm sure that I can stay with—" She stopped before she said Brittany. Her only other friend didn't have a place in her life for Heather's mess. She had her hands full dealing with the fire at her house. "I can stay at a hotel or something."

"You're not staying at a hotel." Kevin set her bag next to the wall, but his movements were awkward and tight. "You're welcome to stay here as long as you need."

"Kevin, I… Thank you." She didn't know what to say. Thank you just didn't seem like enough when what she really wanted to say was that he was part of the reason she had the strength to leave.

He had shown her there could be more in the world; that there could be something besides heartbreak and the constant thoughts that she could be doing something more to make someone else happy, even if that meant being miserable in her own skin.

Kevin had saved her life and he probably didn't even realize it.

She moved toward him. She wanted to take in his scent, the safe edge of soap mixed with the dangerous perfume of smoke. She'd loved that heady mix since she had met him. In truth, she wanted so much more.

For a moment she imagined him lifting her into his arms and taking her to his bedroom…and showing her exactly how good she could feel. She warmed as she imagined his lips running down her body, his hands cupping her curves...

What it would have been like to be utterly his.

She stepped closer, hoping he would wrap his arms around her, pull her in tight and make her feel whole.

He didn't move; instead he looked down the hallway toward the children's rooms. A look of concern flickered over his features.

Lindsay's door was closed and her music was playing, but she could just make out the sounds of his daughter talking on her phone.

"Is Colter home yet?" Heather asked.

Kevin shook his head. "Not yet. He said he's studying."

From his tone, she could tell he was worried.

He looked down at his watch and his face darkened.

"Is everything okay?"

"He should be home by now."

"Don't worry. I'm sure he'll be home soon."

"I'm not. I think he lied to me. I don't think he had any intention of listening. He's been lying a lot lately. But what am I supposed to do?"

She thought of Colter and what his coach had told her. "Has he given you any clues about what is going on with him? Did he break up with a girl or something?"

Kevin finally looked at her. His eyes were filled with a tempest, and as she stared she could have sworn there was a flash of lightning somewhere deep within the squall.

"Colter hasn't talked to me in months." He looked away. "I don't know my own son."

"That's not true, Kevin." She took his hand in hers. "You're a great father."

He shook his head. "No, I'm not. That's the problem. I've been focused on everything except my kids. This week just proved it."

"Stop. That's not true. Just because you're busy doesn't mean you aren't focused on your kids. You do the best you can do."

"Clearly, that isn't enough." He motioned toward Colter's room. "If it was, Colter would be at home or on the baseball field right now, not running off to God-only-knows-where and doing God-only-knows-what."

"Being a parent isn't about being perfect, Kevin. Every teenager goes through a hard time. It's a rite of passage."

"But I don't even know why he's acting out." He walked across the living room to the bookshelves. "I've read all of these stupid things," he said, pointing at the rows of parenting books. "And I still managed to screw it all up."

"No you didn't, Kevin." She followed him across the room. "You have a wonderful daughter and son who love you more than anything. Just because one of them is going through a hard time doesn't make it your fault. I may not know much about parenting, but I know all about guilt. And right now, your guilt isn't helping."

"I can't just stand here and wait for him to come home. What if he's hurt?"

Seeing the anguish on his face, she reached out to him. Her palm cradled his cheek. "If you needed proof you're a good father, there it is, Kevin. If you were as bad a father as you think you are, you wouldn't care. You wouldn't be worried."

"What can I do, Heather? I need to protect him."

She lowered her hand and it felt deprived of him. "Right now you need to trust him. I know it's hard. I know. But he'll come home. When he does, you need to be here for him and, most importantly, you need to talk to him."

His pain was palpable and no matter what she said it didn't seem to subside. In fact, the more she spoke the darker his eyes grew.

"Why does everything have to take a turn for the worst?"

She laughed. "Call me a cynic, but isn't that what life is? Constant upheavals only broken up by quick glimpses of what could be?"

Her face burned as she stared at him and she was struck by her dreams of what "could be."

Some of the darkness in his eyes dissipated. "I don't know what I'd do without you."

"You'd definitely have less to deal with." She smiled.

"That's not true. I would just have to deal with all this alone."

The floodgate seemed to break within him and he rushed to her and took her in his arms. His lips pressed against hers in a glorious cloud of want, the pheromone-laced heat of his tongue flicking against her lower lip, coaxing her to open. His hand moved down her back, his thumb rubbing the skin of her back as it moved lower to her jean-hugged curves.

He pulled back, his forehead against hers, the moisture of his breath dampening her lips. His breath was ragged when he finally spoke. "I know this is wrong, but I've wanted this for so long."

They were the words she longed to hear. No response

she gave him could convey her desire. Instead of speaking, she took hold of the waistband of his black uniform pants and led him down the hall toward his bedroom.

When they entered the darkened room, she locked the door behind them.

Pressing her back against the door, she stopped and stared at him. "I want you, Kevin. I've wanted you for so long."

"Are you sure that you want to do this?"

She wasn't sure of anything the way she sure of that. Her life was in turmoil, rocked by a brutal storm, and the only safe harbor was the one she'd find in this man's arms. She needed to feel him inside her. She needed to know someone cared about her, someone wanted her. If they were going to sleep together, it was a risk, but she couldn't believe it would be a mistake. Not with Kevin.

She nodded at him. "Just be quiet," she said, pushing him down on the bed and climbing on top.

"As you wish." He laughed, pulling her down to him, her body supported by his. His kisses moved down her neck as he lifted up her shirt and then unclasped her bra. Her entire body ached as she yielded to his firm touch and the gentle movement of his lips over her skin.

His hand moved up and he cupped her breast, his thumb gently rubbing over her responding nub, making her desire deepen.

She stood up again so she could open his pants and boxers and, in one swift motion, pull them down his legs and drop them to the floor. His legs were covered in a fine layer of caramel-colored hair and higher up his thigh, the color of his hair darkened.

Kevin unbuttoned her pants. He slipped them down her legs in a slow descent, and with each slip of the fabric he followed with a kiss to her fevered skin. She had never wanted a man like this, not with every cell of her being. And no other man had made her feel what Kevin was making her feel now. For once she felt alive. Her body quaked and heated as Kevin's mouth traveled over her hills and valleys.

He stood up, wrapping his arms around her, and lifted her body to meet his. As she linked her legs behind him, he moved her against the wall, her back pressing against the cold paint, making the heat of him inside her intensify.

She felt guilty about many things, but making love right here, right now was something she'd never regret.

Chapter Eighteen

Kevin ran his finger down Heather's side, tracing the slope of her hip, the naked arc he had always imagined but never thought he would see. Her eyes were closed and her body relaxed under his fingertips. She wasn't asleep, just reveling in the aftermath of a torrid love-making session.

He was a lucky man.

She looked so happy, happier than she had in a long time, and he had made her feel that way.

But she was still married to him.

He pushed back a strand of hair from her neck. She was so beautiful. He would never understand why David had treated her the way he did. How did he not realize what a special woman she was, or how lucky he was to have had her?

If Heather was Kevin's wife, he would never treat her the way David had. He would never cheat, never berate her or call her names. She would be his everything, not something to put down and kick around.

Then again, just because they'd had sex didn't mean that she was his. No. For all he knew, he was just a rebound to her, someone to help her forget about David.

Was it possible she knew about David's infidelity?

He couldn't tell her, but if the arson investigation went to court, it was likely Elke would be called to the stand and her whereabouts would be put to question. She'd have to tell the court where she had been, and with whom. David's secret would be out, and Heather would know Kevin had kept the truth from her.

She'd been lied to enough that, undoubtedly, if she found out he had been keeping it from her, it would be hard to make her understand why. There was no right answer, no right thing to do.

Maybe if he didn't push so hard, and if he listened to Hiller and swept the fires under the rug, it would be for the best. Heather wouldn't have to learn the truth, the chief would be happy and Kevin could concentrate on the kids a little more. If he pulled away from the investigation, maybe it would be for the best.

Then again, if he let it go there was no way of knowing what would happen next. Maybe the arsons would stop. But the feeling in his gut told him there would be more of the same—or worse—especially if the perpetrator made Heather a target now that she'd seen him.

She stirred beside him and for a moment he contemplated turning to her and making love to her again, this time at a slower, less frenzied pace. It was hard not to want it all, especially when she lay relaxed and smiling blissfully beside him.

His phone rang.

He jumped up and grabbed it midring. "Hello?"

"This is Lawrence," the detective said, his voice lower and more hard-edged than usual.

"Everything ready for the meeting?" He stood up and rushed to put his pants back on, then glanced over his shoulder to motion to Heather.

She lay there in bed, her perfect brown-tipped breasts rising and falling as she watched him hurry to get dressed. She frowned, but her expression was playful.

"What are you doing?" Lawrence asked. "You sound...off."

"Nothing. Just had to run home and take care of some urgent business before the meeting." He looked at Heather and smiled.

Heather brushed her hand lazily over her stomach, drawing loose circles around her belly button, reminding Kevin exactly why his mind had turned off and his body had taken over.

He stepped over to her and ran his hand down her naked thigh. Oh, the things he would do to her if life hadn't been waiting.

"Well, there's no need to rush," Lawrence continued.

Kevin looked over at the clock. The meeting was set to start in an hour. "Don't worry. I'm on my way."

"No really, Jensen, there's no need. I'm surprised you haven't heard. Your damned BC got your chief involved—I think he wanted to draw more attention, but the whole thing went up like an atom bomb. Your chief was pissed he wasn't involved and got into it with the mayor. Long story short, the press conference is cancelled. You can thank Hiller."

"You've got to be kidding me. There's an active arsonist and he let his ego get in the way?"

"Hey, this is your department, your chief and your BC, not mine." Lawrence chuckled. "Just let me know when I can bring over the marshmallows."

"What?"

"Yeah, I want to be prepared for the next arson. Hate to let a good fire go to waste."

"I'll let you know." He clicked off his phone and threw it down on the bed.

Damn that Hiller. He'd been against Kevin from the very beginning. Kevin should have known he would pull some kind of stunt.

"Everything okay?" Heather asked, pulling the sheet over her naked body.

"Don't do that," he pleaded. "That's the only thing going right." He pulled the sheet down, sat down beside her and ran his fingers over the sharp line of her collarbone.

"This spot," he said, stopping at the intersection of the clavicle and the shoulder where a soft little indentation hugged his fingertip. "This spot's mine." He leaned down and kissed her porcelain skin.

She said nothing as she ran her hands through his hair.

"I know I don't have any rights to, but—"

She sat up and pressed her lips to his, stopping him from finishing his sentence.

"Shut up, Kevin. Just shut up," she said, leaning back. She looked at him with the same expression she'd had while they were making love—soft, open and comforting.

Her breasts reminded him of all the other curves of her body, and all he wanted to do was fall back into her.

"Now, how can I help you?"

He smiled as he looked at her, but he let it fall away as he thought of the storm that waited for him outside of his bedroom door. "Detective Lawrence and I had put together a press conference to pull our arsonist out of the shadows, and then Hiller, the battalion chief who had worked on the cases—you met him at Brittany's—stepped in and the whole thing was canned."

He sighed. "Now I've got no suspect, no press conference, a missing son and a pissed-off battalion chief, chief and mayor. I'll be lucky if I don't get suspended—or worse."

"Why would Hiller want to get your conference cancelled? I don't get it. Wouldn't he want to catch whoever is behind these arsons just as much as you do?"

"You'd think so, but you know politics. Hiller and the chief are more worried about the financials than keeping people safe. If we keep this an open investigation it's going to cost the department money it doesn't have."

"But aren't they worried about it happening again?"

"Sure, but so far no one's been hurt. They're trying to argue against spending money on investigating little fires where the insurance companies will cover everything. Even if I nail down the perpetrator, the district attorney probably isn't going to take the case to trial. Knowing how Montana works, the guy will get a plea bargain and some slap-on-the-wrist sentence."

Heather nodded. "So why don't you just call it off?"

"Call what off?"

"Your investigation."

"I guess it would be easiest if I did. The honest truth is that a lot of the time it just feels like I'm phoning my job in. After Allison died, I couldn't..." He paused as he searched for the right words. "I couldn't be the man I had been. But this investigation was my chance, my opportunity to show not only the department, but the city and my family that I can stop bad things from happening. I may not have been able to save Allison, but maybe I can save someone else."

She sat up and wrapped her arms around him. "You can't feel guilty about Allison. You *couldn't* save her, not even the doctors could. You don't need to carry that weight."

He looked at her through teary eyes. "But I do. I have. This is my chance to make it—and me—better."

She reached up and cupped his face. "Then you need to fight for this. You need to do what you think is right. Don't let me or anyone stop you."

He reached up and took her hands in his, pulling them from his face. Her fingers wrapped around his hands as he lifted them to his mouth and softly kissed her skin.

"I can watch Lindsay and wait here for Colter. You go. When you get back, I'll be here waiting for you and *this*." She sat forward and kissed his lips.

He stood up, carefully putting distance between him and his dreams of something more.

"I'll be back soon. Why don't your order some pizza? And—" he paused as he carefully selected his words "—just so we don't confuse my kids, there's a spare bedroom downstairs. As much as I want you to stay here with me, I think it would be best for now if you stayed down there. Okay?"

She sat back against his wooden headboard and her face tightened. "That's fine."

"I'm sorry, it's just—"

"No. It's fine. I get it." She slid her legs out from the sheets and reached for her perfect pink panties. As soon as she slipped them up her legs, he wanted to pull them off again, but he resisted.

"I'll see you when I get home?"

"Yep. I'll be here. Lindsay needs me."

He had made a mistake. Kevin saw it in her eyes the moment he closed the bedroom door, but now it was too late to go back and make things right. He stood in the hallway and looked back at his room. There was nothing he could say that would make things better.

If they were caught, Lindsay would probably be okay about their "sleepover," but the same couldn't be said of Colter. Kevin was already having enough problems with his son; he didn't need to stoke the fire.

He stopped in front of Colter's door. After a momentary hesitation he twisted the cold metal knob. The room was a mess and it stunk of dirty shoes, teenage boy and the sulfur-rich scent of rotting food. A plate littered with unidentifiable food sat on his desk next to a glass of what must have been milk. He made his way over to the plate; at least he could take it to the kitchen and drop the stinking mess into the sink.

The desk was covered in a mess of candy wrappers, but near the top of the stack of papers was a receipt from Truck Boys, the local auto parts store. Picking up the receipt, Kevin read the items:

Mechanix Gloves…$14.99
TB Brake Fluid…$4.97

He gripped the back of the desk chair to steady himself.

Why would Colter need to buy brake fluid? He hadn't mentioned his car needing supplies.

His mind raced as he thought back to the night of Elke's fire. As usual these days, he and Colter had been at odds, maybe more so than usual, but was it possible Colter had snuck out in the night to start a fire?

He looked at the date of the receipt. It was marked the day before Elke's fire. The next day, Kevin had found his money missing; Colter had probably taken it the night before. Plus, the day of Brittany's fire, Colter had bailed on his morning classes.

Kevin carefully folded the receipt and slipped it into his pocket. Sure there were some connections, but none of it was more than circumstantial. Colter didn't fit the profile of the man Elke's neighbors had seen walking away from the fire, but Mrs. Jones *had* admitted it was dark and she hadn't seen the man's face. As much as he hated the thought, there was a chance Colter could be the arsonist. With a father in the department, he certainly had enough resources to learn how to make a chemical fire.

Maybe he needed to feel in control. Maybe the fires were set to get back at him.

Kevin walked toward the mess of clothes on the floor and picked up one of Colter's discarded shoes—size ten.

No...

Colter would never do something so stupid.

He'd never try to hurt anyone.

Not his son.

Chapter Nineteen

Heather buttoned her shirt as she glanced into Kevin's bathroom mirror. She'd washed up and dressed, and except for the new ache in her gut, everything was as it had been just a few hours before.

The front door shut and Kevin's truck roared to life.

She slipped out of his bedroom and into the hall. Lindsay's music was playing and Heather tapped on her door. "Lindsay?"

A crescendo of her footsteps moved toward the door. She opened it a crack and looked out. "Huh?"

"Everything okay?"

"Yeah, I'm fine, just watching videos on YouTube. You should've seen this one I just watched. The cat can *actually* talk. I swear. It says 'no' and you would swear it was a person. Wanna see it?"

Heather laughed. "Sure."

Lindsay opened the door and, taking her hand, led her to the computer. She clicked a button and a gray cat took over the screen.

The cat started to caterwaul, but Heather barely paid attention; instead she couldn't take her gaze off Lindsay. As Lindsay watched the silly cat, her eyes bright-ened and she laughed from a deep place in her belly, the sound so rich that Heather couldn't resist joining her.

The sound was so strange. It had been so long since she'd heard that specific sound—real, true delight.

For a moment, Heather imagined her life being just like this. She and Kevin could get married; they could raise Lindsay and Colter together. They could be each other's rocks.

The front door opened and slammed shut.

"Kevin, is that you?" She stood up and patted Lindsay on the shoulder. "Have fun, kiddo. I'll be right in the living room if you need me."

"Okay, Mrs. Sampson." Lindsay didn't look away from the cat.

Heather closed the girl's door as she made her way down the hall.

Standing in the middle of the living room was David. His eyes were bloodshot, as if he had been crying.

"David, what's the matter?"

"I made a mistake, Kitten."

She cringed as he used her pet name. "What do you mean?" She tried to steel herself. He wasn't the type to admit any wrongdoing.

"What did Kevin tell you?" He stepped closer to her, forcing her to take a step back.

"He didn't tell me anything."

David looked away from her, but not before she noticed a slight smirk flash over his face.

"What did you do? Is there something Kevin should've told me about?"

David paused for a second. "I… He came over and… then…" He looked around the room as if somewhere in the air hung the words he was looking for.

"What, David?" She crossed her arms over her chest.

"I told him about the divorce," David said, glancing at her with the puppy-dog eyes he always used when he rounded this curve in his emotional cycle—the same abusive cycle she fell for every time.

"I told him how bad I felt. I never should've asked for the divorce."

"What?" The word came out no louder than a breath as the floor seemed to disappear from beneath her.

He couldn't be serious.

"I'm sorry, Kitten. I made a mistake. Come home."

David had to be kidding. He had been thoughtless, sadistic and unforgivably cruel.

"No, David."

He reached out for her and took her hand. She started to pull away from his grip but stopped. If she acted petulant, he would know what she had done. He always knew when she had done something wrong. If she wanted to get anything in the divorce, he could never find out about her tryst with Kevin.

"*No* what, Kitten? You wouldn't refuse me. You love me." He stepped closer and draped her arms around him and pulled her close against him. His chest was warm against her cheek, so warm it made her start to sweat.

She pushed him away. She had loved him when they'd first met, when she had known him as a man of integrity, a man who wanted to help people. He was no longer that man. He was something far more sinister and manipulative.

"You're wrong. I don't love you."

He laughed, the sound dangerous. "Come on now. We both know that isn't true. You're just mad. I get it.

But please… You know I go crazy like this every once in a while. You know how bad I feel."

"If you feel so bad, then why do you keep treating me like this?"

David took her face in his hands. "I don't know, Kitten. I'm sorry. I wish I could be perfect for you. I do. You deserve the best, but sometimes you just make me so mad. Maybe it's the stress of work. Maybe it's the fear you'll leave me that makes me want to push you away first. Who knows? All I know is that I want you to take me back."

He rubbed his thumbs over her temples, the motion both placating and annoying.

She reached up and took hold of his hands, trying to move them from her face, but he held strong.

"I know you live for me," he said with a sick smile.

She gripped his hands hard. He had meant the words as some kind of compliment, but behind them she could read what he really meant—she couldn't live without him. More than that—that she wasn't good enough for anyone else.

Her father had been the same way with her mother. They had constantly fought, mostly about money, but even as a child Heather had known there was something just under the surface—there was always some kind of hidden meaning behind the words her father had spoken. Now here she was, reliving the same fights, the same berating behavior and the same phases of abuse that her mother had gone through. She was perpetuating the cycle.

"What do you want from our relationship?"

"I know I always said I wanted kids, but the last few days I've been thinking and I don't know if it's right for me. I mean look at Kevin," he said, motioning around the living room. "He has his hands full. Brittany told me about what's happening with Colter. I don't want to have to deal with everything that comes with kids. Think about it. If we bypass the whole thing, we could spend our time and money doing what we really want— we could travel, we could get lost in the world."

"Kids are something I *really* want, David."

"Why? They just eat, poop and destroy everything."

She stepped back from him and turned to go. She didn't want this... She didn't want him. Kevin waited.

"Wait, Kitten, if you want kids... Fine. Whatever. Just come home. You have to come home. If you don't... I don't know what I'll do," he said, with a dangerous edge to his words.

She turned back to him. His face was tight and he glared at her—his expression almost bloodthirsty.

Her gut tightened. He hadn't meant he would *hurt* her, had he?

"You... Why are you threatening me?"

"I'm not threatening you," he said with an alarming laugh. "I'd never threaten you, Kitten." He reached out and took her arm and gave it a tight, painful squeeze. "You'd never make me go that far. Would you?"

She tried to pull out of his grip, but he only gripped harder, making her arm throb with pain.

She had to stay with him. If she didn't, it was clear from the look in his eye that he would do whatever he needed to do to keep her from leaving him.

"I can't leave Lindsay here by herself," she said in a panic.

"Where did Kevin go?"

"Why are you worried about where Kevin is, David?"

He smiled the smile of a politician. "Don't worry your pretty little head about it."

She hated when David spoke down to her like that, like she couldn't think for herself.

David pinched the back of her arm, as if he was measuring her. "You know, Kitten, you could lose a little weight. You aren't what you used to be." He looked her up and down, stopping for a second at the little roll of skin that spilled over the waist of her jeans.

She recoiled from him.

He was such a jerk.

"If that's true, David, I don't know why you want me to come back."

He pinched her arm. "You know, if you were easier to live with, none of this would've happened. This is all your fault. I've tried my best to get you back. If you walk away, you won't be under my protection any more. You won't be safe. You'll never be safe. You'll have no one."

Her skin crawled as his words scuttled over her. She had to play along at least until she knew she was out of danger.

She turned back to him. "If I come home, you need to prove to me you're going to change. You have to be nicer. And I'm going to need access to everything. You can't go on controlling my life."

He tilted his head and smiled. "Kitten, everything will be fine as long as we can just put this divorce talk behind us."

"I'll get Lindsay and have her come over and wait with us until Kevin gets home." Her throat tightened

as she said Kevin's name. He would never understand
what she was doing or why, but he'd never lived with
David. He didn't understand how terrifying he could be.

Chapter Twenty

Every time Kevin closed his eyes, he was back in bed with Heather. Her long brown hair lay around her in a halo as if she was his personal angel. It had been so long since he'd been with a woman; in fact, the last woman had been Allison.

For a moment, he wished he was eighteen again and he could just appreciate the moment with Heather without adding the weight of all of his baggage. Nothing in life was easy anymore.

He reached for his phone and tried to call Colter again.

This time, his voice mail was full.

When he found him, Colter was going to be in trouble.

He looked over at the clipboard in the passenger seat of the truck and thought about the receipt he'd stuck inside—the evidence his son might not be the boy he'd thought he was.

He gripped the steering wheel tight as he drove toward the fire station.

There was no way Colter could be the arsonist. Sure, he knew Brittany, but Colter didn't know Elke. Did he?

Even if he did know the waitress, that meant nothing. His son didn't have a reason to pull some stunt like this. It didn't make any sense. It just didn't fit.

Then again, he couldn't dispute the receipt. He had proof Colter had bought the same brake fluid used in the fires immediately prior to the arson. He had the same size feet. But so far everything was circumstantial, even the fact his son wasn't accounted for at the time of the ignition. Then again, at a certain point, when everything was pointing one way, there was usually only one answer.

If he had just had his life together, if he had just been a better father, none of this would have happened. He wouldn't have a son that was a criminal. If he could have helped him, he could have stopped Colter from going down this road.

He pulled the truck into the parking lot of the station. Through the sliding glass doors he could see Hiller sitting in the lounge, his feet up on the ottoman as Kevin parked. He needed to file his findings, but if he put his most recent notes into the computer, the department would have access. If he put in his thoughts about Colter, everyone would know his son was a suspect before tomorrow's breakfast.

Hiller turned in his chair and, noticing him in the parking lot, got up and opened the door.

Screw it.

He threw the truck into Reverse. Hiller could wait, filing the papers could wait, but his son couldn't. He couldn't let his thoughts about his son's guilt go any further. It was his job to keep his family safe, even if that meant just getting to them first.

He hit the gas and sped out of the parking lot.

As he raced down the road, he dialed Colter's best

friend, Shawn. He glanced down at the time. Shawn was probably still at the baseball game, but it was worth a shot.

He wasn't surprised when the phone went to voice mail. He hung up without leaving a message. Shawn wasn't the type to rat out his friend anyway. If Kevin didn't find Colter by dark, he would call again. Heck, he'd show up at Shawn's door.

He drove toward the high school. Maybe Colter was under the bleachers with some girl. Maybe that was what all this was about, why he was so secretive. Maybe he was using his testosterone to do his thinking. Whatever it was, when Kevin found him, they were going to have a long talk.

The school parking lot was mostly empty. The only cars were parked near the baseball fields and a few were scattered in the teacher's lot. Colter's blue 1994 Honda Accord was nowhere to be seen.

He drove around back and turned down the little alley that led to the rear of the building. The doors leading to the kitchens were closed, but the auto shop's garage door was open. Inside, up on the car lift, was Colter's Honda. The big industrial-strength lights were on under the car's undercarriage. In the spotlight was Colter, his coveralls spotted with black grease and a wrench in his hand.

Kevin parked his truck in front of the garage doors and got out. "Why didn't you answer your phone?"

Colter turned, giving him a confused expression. "Huh? Dad? What're you doing here? Aren't you supposed to be at a meeting?"

"I'm here because you don't answer your phone. Everyone has been worried about you. *I've* been worried about you. I thought you were studying for a Spanish test."

Colter walked out from under the car and wiped his hands on a shop rag. "I didn't tell you cause I thought you'd take it...well, just about as well as you are."

"I'm pissed because I didn't know where you were."

"One way or another, Dad, I was at school. It wasn't a complete lie. You don't have to be so pissed."

"Why didn't you answer your damn phone?" Kevin tried to pull back his temper, but there were still so many unanswered questions.

"Are you really going to come down on me? You're the one who's never available. So sue me that I decided I wasn't gonna sit around and wait for you so we could talk about me getting pulled from the game."

Kevin walked into the shop and put his hand up on the car's tire. "I had no idea where you were. Do you know how worried I was about you? How worried I *am* about you?"

"Wait, Dad. If that's true, tell me, did you even *remember* I had a game today?"

"Of course I remembered."

"Did you stop by?"

Kevin felt swamped by guilt.

"You didn't. Did you?" Colter threw down the wrench in the box of tools with a loud clang. "I can't believe you didn't even bother to show up for the game. You don't care, so why should I?"

Kevin's anger melted away. "I do care, bud. That's why I'm here. Don't quit chasing your dreams because of me. You're not a quitter. You're an amazing baseball player and a good student. We just need to work together to get you back on the right track."

"You think I'm good?"

"I think you're awesome, bud. You're just making some bad choices." Kevin sighed. "Tell me, what's going on with you?"

"You mean why did I get benched?"

"If that's what you want to talk about. Yeah, what led up to that?"

Colter turned his back to him and picked up a few different tools, as though he was looking for exactly the right one to get him out of this jam.

Kevin waited, but Colter didn't answer.

"Okay, bud, let's restart. Why did you steal money from me? All you ever have to do is ask and I'll give you what you need."

Colter turned to look at him. "I didn't mean to steal your money. I've just been trying to fix my car. I was hoping I could get it fixed before you found out about it. I didn't want you to get mad."

"Is this where you were the other day when the attendance secretary called?"

Colter nodded.

"If you were skipping to work on your car, why did you to lie to me and tell me you were in class?"

"Well… Okay, yeah. It was a lie, but I didn't want to tell you my car broke down."

"Again, Colter, if you just tell me the truth, I won't get upset. But all these lies… How can I trust you when you've been lying to me?"

"You have to trust me, Dad. I had to replace the lines. That's why I needed your money."

"Where were you on Wednesday morning?"

"At school."

"How about before school?"

In all honesty, Colter could have been gone in the hours the fire took place and he wouldn't have known. If Colter was pressed in court for a strict timeline, there would be little Kevin could do to corroborate.

"You promise me you didn't go anywhere before school, and the only day you skipped was the day you went to Truck Boys for brake fluid and when you were working on your car?"

"Wait a minute. I didn't tell you I went to Truck Boys."

He waved him off. "Did you go anywhere else? It's important you tell me the truth, Colter. Very important."

Colter looked down at the floor. "How do you know?"

His gut tightened. "Just tell me what you did, Colter. I can't help you if you don't tell me the truth."

Colter looked up. "Fine. I skipped some of my classes over the past few weeks. Shawn and I have been going up to Deep Creek to go mudding. I just… I didn't think it would mess with my baseball."

"You went mudding with this car?" No wonder the thing had broken down.

"Yes, sir." Colter stared at the wrench in his hand. "I know it was stupid."

Colter had lied so many times—was it possible he was lying again? Was he trying to cover up the fact that he'd committed a crime?

"But you were at school part of the time this week?"

"Yeah, I was here most of the week. After I tore up the lines, it wasn't like I could keep going up there. I just missed a couple of hours to run to the auto parts store, and yesterday I skipped English to go to Taco Bell with Shawn. I was hoping I could get it fixed and make up my classes before semifinals, but Mr. T found out I skipped more classes so he benched me."

"I hope you learned your lesson." Kevin shook his head as he heard his own father's words coming out of his mouth.

"I'm sorry, Dad. I shouldn't have hidden it from you."

Kevin stepped next to Colter and drew him into his arms. "Bud, I love you. We all make mistakes. God knows I have. I'm sorry, too. I promise I'll try harder to be available."

For a moment all he could think about was the afternoons Colter had waited for him on the porch. For a split second, he was back there and Colter was five years old and clinging to him.

Colter stepped back. "I got to get this fixed, Dad."

Kevin nodded. "Sure, but one more thing… Can you promise me you weren't at Elke Goldstein's house the morning of her fire?"

"Who's Elke Goldstein? What are you talking about, Dad?" Colter frowned.

"Where were you the day of Brittany's fire? About 1:00 p.m.?"

Colter frowned. "That's when Shawn and I skipped to go to lunch."

"So you were never near her house?"

Colter looked away, picked up a hammer and spun it in his hands. "Actually, I did come home."

"So you drove by her house around one?"

Colter nodded. "Yeah, but I didn't stop. There was something weird."

"What?"

"Well, on the way home we passed one of your guys' trucks."

No one had arrived on scene until one-thirty. It's not possible one of the city's fire trucks was there before.

"Was that about one-thirty?"

Colter shook his head. "Nope, I had Chemistry at one-thirty. I was back in time. Had to be before."

Kevin's hands shook. "Did you see who was driving?"

"Well, that's the weird part. I'm pretty sure it was one of the guys you work with, but when I waved, the guy didn't seem to see me."

Chapter Twenty-One

Heather rolled her suitcase to the bottom of the steps, but instead of taking it up to her and David's bedroom, she dropped the bag by the landing.

Lindsay walked into the living room. "I'm going to go outside and play. Okay, Mrs. Sampson?" She looked back over her shoulder at David, her lip quivering slightly.

As much as Heather wanted to reach out to Lindsay, she knew it was best to let her go.

"That's fine."

As the door clicked shut behind Lindsay, David walked up behind Heather. "When are you going to cut those kids loose? Lindsay's old enough that she doesn't need a babysitter, or a nanny, or whatever you are."

"I don't want to *cut them loose*. I love those kids."

"That's stupid, Kitten. They're not even your kids. You don't mean anything to them. You are just setting yourself up to get your heart broken."

"No." She paused. "No... That's not what matters. What matters is that they know they have someone who loves them, someone who will always be there when they have a problem." She glanced out the back window and watched as Lindsay sat on the swing. The previous owner had installed a play gym in the yard, and Heather hadn't had the heart to take it down. She'd always hoped one day her child would find it a perfect place to play.

"I love you so much. No one could ever love you as much as I do," David whispered.

He took her by the waist. She flinched under his touch.

"No, David." She pushed his hands off. "Stop."

"What? Doesn't it make you happy that I want you? That I wanted you to come home? Didn't I show you I was sorry when I came to get you?"

"That's what I don't get, David. Why did you come to get me?"

"Because I wanted you. I needed you."

"But why, David? And don't tell me you suddenly just decided you love me. If you loved me, you would never have left a note to tell me you were leaving. You never would've treated me the way you have."

"You are so damn frustrating." He took a step back.

"And you think you are some kind of daisy to live with? You don't think I get frustrated with you? But you don't see me walking out that door at the first sign of trouble. You don't see me leaving you notes."

"You would never leave me. Come on, where would you go?"

"I'm stronger than you think."

He tried to reach out toward her, but she batted his hand away. "Kitten, I never said you weren't strong. That's one of the reasons I fell for you." He gave her a placating smile. "When I first met you, you were so vibrant, so full of life…"

"And now?" She should've never asked the question, but from the way he spoke it was obvious that he wanted to deliver the blow.

"You know. You've changed. It's like your light or something has gone out. That's why—"

"You left me," she said, finishing his sentence.

He looked her in the eyes. "I just want you to be the girl I once knew."

She thought about all the times he had put her down, the times he had called her stupid, fat and lazy… Those were the moments that a little bit of her died. And now, when push came to shove, it was her fault she had changed?

"Thanks to you, David, that girl is gone." She held his gaze.

David looked away. "You're pissed. I get it, Kitten. Why don't you go upstairs, take a little nap and we'll talk about this later?" He gave a smug chuckle.

Her hands balled into tight fists. She wasn't stupid, and that was something he was never going to understand.

Confronting him again wasn't worth the fight. He was too narcissistic to care how she felt, or to try to understand what he did that bothered her. Nothing was ever his fault.

"Don't bother coming upstairs tonight. The door will be locked." She turned away from him, leaving David to stand guppy-mouthed and blabbering things she didn't bother to hear.

She made her way outside. Lindsay sat on the swing, her feet digging into the dirt, creating little clouds of dust as she swung.

"You okay, honey?" Heather asked, sitting down in the swing next to her.

"Yeah." The tone of her voice made it clear she wasn't.

"You know, you can always talk to me. I'm here for you."

Lindsay looked toward the door, where David stood at the window, staring out at them.

"Why does everything have to be so hard?" Lindsay shifted in the swing, making the chain clang.

Heather sighed. "I'm sorry you keep seeing the worst between David and me. We're going through some tough stuff right now, but it's almost over."

"I know. He doesn't make you happy... Not like when you're with my daddy. I love watching you with Daddy. You look so pretty. You're always smiling."

Heather stared at the girl.

Out of the mouth of babes...

"Would you be okay with it if I was your daddy's girlfriend?"

Lindsay rushed to her and threw her arms around her. "Colter and I have talked about it... We've always wanted you to be our mommy. We'd be a whole family."

THE COLD CHEESE pizza sat on the island as Lindsay, David and Heather sat watching *Frozen*. Lindsay's body was pressed against Heather, and she had her arm wrapped lovingly around her.

David's phone beeped with a text message. He looked almost relieved as he read the screen. He glanced over at Heather. "I have to run to work. Looks like I have a late-fifties male with possible CHF coming in from the ER."

"Go ahead," Heather said, thankful that with his departure some of the tension would go with him, as well.

He ran upstairs and, a few minutes later, made his way out through the garage without a good-bye.

Heather gave Lindsay a hug. "Want any more pizza?"

Lindsay shook her head, her attention still on the movie.

She never wanted to lose this—the time with Lindsay. It was just too bad Colter wasn't there, and Kevin. If they were, she would have everything she needed to be happy.

There was a knock at the door.

Getting up, she made her way over and opened the door. Almost as if thinking of them had beckoned them to her, Kevin and his son stood on the front porch. Kevin's arm was over Colter's shoulders.

"Hiya, Mrs. Sampson," Colter said with a smile. "Sorry you were worried about me—I was at school working on a project. And sorry I forgot to tell you about the game."

She looked at Kevin, who gave her a reassuring nod.

"I'm just glad you're okay. Is everything all right with baseball?"

He nodded, but looked to Kevin.

"We're going to talk to his teachers about doing some makeup work and then try to make things right with his coach. I'm sure we can get him back on track for college and the Huskies. Right, Colt?" He squeezed Colter's shoulders in a side hug.

Colter smiled, his eyes lighting up with his father's hope.

"Why don't you guys come in?" Heather asked, motioning toward the couch and Lindsay.

Kevin frowned. "I thought you were going to be staying at our place for a while?"

She looked away. "Well…yeah… David came over and apologized. I—"

"Oh." Kevin took a step back from her. "I get it."

"No. It's not like that," she said, but Kevin's smile disappeared.

"Lindsay," Kevin called. "We need to get going. Mrs. Sampson's probably tired."

"You don't need to go. I wanted to talk to you."

"Actually, I do need to go, Heather." He finally looked at her, but all the softness was gone from his eyes. "My family needs me."

She stopped. He needed to be with his family, to fix things that needed to be fixed, and no matter how badly she wanted to be a part of their lives she couldn't. David had been right—they weren't her family.

"How about coffee tomorrow?" she urged, trying to stop Kevin from thinking the worst.

"Fine. Text me, but as you know, I'm kind of busy. I may not be able to drop everything." His tone whipped through the air between them, lashing her with his words' true meaning—he regretted sleeping with her.

"Oh... Okay," she mumbled.

Lindsay walked outside and Kevin turned away.

"See you later, Mrs. Sampson," Colter called into the night.

She waved after them, but they weren't even out of sight before the loneliness crept in.

THE BED WAS cold when she finally slipped between the sheets, but the chill of the bed was something she had long ago grown used to. At least she hadn't had to follow through on locking David out of the bedroom; no, he hadn't even bothered to come home.

It was funny, the second he thought she had come back into his life, he had slipped back into his old habits. If she stayed it wouldn't be long before she received another note.

David's side of the bed was a sea of white. His pillow was fluffed, but there were tiny wrinkles where his head had lain. The loneliness crept a little deeper.

This feeling, this emptiness in her center, was something she was going to have to get used to. Maybe with therapy, she could learn to get through this…or better, learn to be happy being by herself.

Happy being by myself…

As the thought echoed in her mind, she reached over, picked up David's pillow and threw it to the floor.

I don't want to be by myself. I want to be with Kevin.

Yet, until she was healthy, she couldn't pull him any deeper into her life. Maybe after the divorce was finalized and she'd gone through therapy, maybe then she would be ready. Maybe then, she could not just make him happy, but have the strength to be happy with herself.

She smiled as she moved her body into the no-man's-land that was the center of the bed. She stretched out her arms and legs like Da Vinci's *Vitruvian Man*. Snuggling deeper, her foot touched something silky.

She threw back the comforter and sheets. Tucked deep in the bed's corner on David's side was a tiny wad of black fabric. She picked it up, and the satin unfurled revealing a woman's G-string.

Heather jumped out of bed and dropped the panties. She hadn't owned a G-string since…well, never.

Unless David was experimenting with women's clothing, she had her evidence for an equitable divorce.

She took a picture on her phone and sent it to Ms.

Kohl with a note: Found these in my bed. Evidence of David's cheating. Prenup nullified?

She ran downstairs and got a plastic bag and a pair of tongs. When she got back to her bed, she picked up the disgusting panties with the silver tongs and stuffed them into the bag. The black plastic-wrapped *thing* looked out of place as she dropped it onto his dresser.

Next she pulled the sheets from the bed, letting them fall to the floor. She could deal with the mess in the morning.

Lugging a new blanket and pillow from the closet, she lay down on the unmade bed. As she slipped away to sleep, she couldn't help but think about how her life was just like the bed—full of secrets, lies and defilement...and it, too, had been left in total disarray.

Chapter Twenty-Two

He looked down at Heather Sampson as he pulled the matchbox from his pocket. The box dropped from his hand, spilling matches on her bedroom floor in a heap of deadly promise. Crouching down, he scooped them back into the container, careful to move quietly, afraid that at any second she would awaken and find him standing over her.

Her eyes were closed and her lips slightly parted, as if she waited for a kiss from her Prince Charming. She should have known better. There was no such thing as Prince Charming. There were only toads and a precious few men like him—men who worked to make everything just.

The sad truth was that there was no justice in marriage—at least not in any of the marriages he had witnessed. No. Marriage was one lie after another. One hurt feeling masked with a fake smile, only to have another lie strip it away. It was an endless cycle of pain.

What was the point? What was it all for?

As far as he could tell, it was for nothing more than ego and some idealistic hope that if they acted happy, if they faked it well enough, maybe they could finally believe it themselves.

He was here to make her a martyr, not that she would understand, but this was his chance to show her and the world what her marriage truly was—nothing more than smoke and ashes. A fire that had yet to burn itself out. But at last the time had come. The hour was here for him to stoke the flames and let them consume every crumb of her failing marriage.

The inferno could have it all.

He walked out of her bedroom and made his way downstairs where the glorious scent of gasoline filled the space. Unlike the others, Heather's house would go up in a flash. In one giant fireball the whole charade would be over—the secrets, the lies, the fake smiles and hurt feelings. It would all be gone, and all her pain could be for a higher purpose.

The night air blew into the house, diluting the gas's perfume. He made sure to leave the door open as he stepped out and walked toward the garage. A puddle of gas sat on the sidewalk, just waiting for him.

He struck the match.

It was so much easier this way.

The fire's smoke curled skyward, creating a trail that led to the heavens. If he had his way, life would be better and she would be free.

THE AIR WAS thick with smoke, choking Heather as she rolled from the bed and onto the floor. Flames licked up the walls as her smoke detectors screeched.

She screamed, hoping someone would hear.

Stay calm. I have to stay calm. I need to save my oxygen. I need to get out of here.

Her knees rubbed against the hot carpet as she

crawled toward the door. A path of fire ran through the middle of the door frame, blocking her way. The only other way out of the room was through the window, but it would be a two-story fall.

Her body froze with indecision. No one was going to come for her. She was going to die. Right here. Right now.

Tears spilled down her cheeks.

I don't want to die...

The lights flickered around her and went out, leaving her alone in smoky darkness.

She forced herself to move across the floor. She drew in a breath of the tarry smoke and the heat of it penetrated her lungs, seeming to cook her from the inside. Her mind blurred, as if she was choking, not breathing.

If she didn't hurry, the gases and heat would kill her.

Just keep moving...

The alarms blared overhead, barely audible above the roar of the fire.

She hurried by the flames in the doorway, careful to keep out of reach of their touch. The fire cascaded down the top of the steps and spilled up the walls.

Someone wanted her dead.

She couldn't let them win.

The stairs were too steep and the flames too close for her to crawl down, but if she stood, her head would be in the deadly smoke.

She crouched as she tried not to inhale the black haze that filled the stairwell. She rushed down the stairs, carefully avoiding the line of fire. Reaching the bottom, she got back onto her hands and knees.

Her lungs ached as she pulled in a deep breath of sooty air.

The living room was black, but the front door had to be close.

If she could just reach the door.

Her hands searched the floor that in daylight was familiar but, in the blinding darkness, seemed like the surface of the moon. Her hand brushed a hot wall to her right.

The stairwell didn't reach the wall where the front door was located. If she was going to have a chance of getting out, she would have to cross the floor…and keep from getting disoriented.

She had to move. The smoke was getting thicker. Soon there would be no air left to breathe.

She crawled low in the direction of the door. The metal door was warm, but she pulled it open, pulling fresh air into the room. The cloud of smoke and flames rolled out over her as it searched for more oxygen. She rushed outside into the night. The heat followed her like a grasping hand, wanting to pull her back into the deadly furnace.

The street was empty. The only lights were from the streetlamps. No one knew. No one had seen what was happening to her.

She ran to Kevin's house and banged on the front door.

"Kevin!" she screamed.

The door opened and Kevin stood there, his eyes wide and alert. "What's the matter?"

"My house is on fire!" She pointed toward her house as smoke roiled from the front door.

"Get inside. I'll call 911." He turned and ran to the

phone and dialed as she followed him into the house. He talked fast to the operator, his words muted and monotone.

She leaned against the wall by the door, her body numb with shock.

He hung up the phone and walked toward her. "Sit down." He took her by the arm and led her to the couch.

The leather was cold against her skin, making her scorched flesh burn.

"Are you okay?" he asked, getting down on his knees in front of her.

"It was so hot."

"You're okay. Everything's okay." He looked over her arms, turning them as he looked for serious burns. "I *knew* I shouldn't have left you alone… Damn it. Does anything hurt?"

"I'm fine."

"Where's David?"

She started to speak, but her words turned into a jumbled mess as her tears took over. Had David done this to her? Had he acted on his threat?

He wrapped her in his arms. Her face pressed into his neck as she sobbed and her body shook with terror.

"You're okay. You're with me," he whispered. "I have you. You're safe with me."

Chapter Twenty-Three

If David was behind this, he was going to kill him with his bare hands.

Kevin dialed the number for the front desk of the Heart Center.

"Hello, Community Medical Center Heart Center, this is Patty. How may I direct your call?"

"Hi, Patty. I need to talk to Dr. Sampson."

"One moment, please." The line switched to elevator music that sounded like something from a funeral home.

Finally the line clicked back. "May I ask who is calling, please?"

"This is Inspector Jensen with the Missoula Fire Department."

"Well, Inspector, Dr. Sampson is currently in surgery."

"How long has he been in there?"

"Well, due to HIPAA regulations—"

"I don't care about the patient... Well, I do, but I just care how long he's been in surgery. It's important."

"I, uh... Well, he's been in there for at least the past three hours."

David wasn't his man.

"Thank you, Patty."

"Would you like me to give him a message?"

"Tell him his house is on fire."

He clicked the phone off and stepped out in front of the house. The firefighters had arrived and now struggled to gain control of the blaze. The windows of Heather's house were gone and flames licked up the siding.

A few feet from him, he saw Lindsay wrap her arms around Heather's waist as Colter stepped to her side. "I'm sorry, Mrs. Sampson."

She nodded. "Call me Heather, guys."

Lindsay hugged her tighter.

If Kevin had his way, they would call her something else entirely, but Heather wasn't ready for such a commitment. No, she had moved back in with David...not long after they had made love. He just didn't understand how she could go back to her old life and a man like David.

Then again, when she'd run from the fire, it wasn't David she had run to.

Her jaw was set as she watched her house burn. She was so strong. If he had been through everything she had, he would've been at the bottom of some bottle— or worse.

Hiller pulled up to the house and, when he noticed him, gave Kevin a shallow dip of the head.

"You guys stay here. I need to handle something," Kevin said.

Heather nodded, but as she looked at him, he could see the tired circles under her eyes. Whoever did this to her, whoever was responsible for hurting her, was going down.

He walked over to Hiller as he stepped out of his truck.

"Guys say it looks like arson. Liquid accelerants, huh?" Hiller asked.

"What took you so long to get here?"

Hiller grabbed his notebook and stepped past him, barely glancing at him. "Are you really going to talk to me about being on time, Mr. King-of-the-Barbecue?"

"That was different and you know it. This time a woman's life was at stake. Heather could've died."

"But she didn't."

"Yeah, and we're just lucky." Kevin shoved his fists into his pockets in an effort to stop him from hitting the BC.

"You know, Jensen, you've a hell of a reputation when it comes to women."

"What's that supposed to mean?"

"Well, look at you. Any woman you have in your life seems to be doomed. First your wife…now Heather." Hiller motioned toward her.

Kevin drew his fist tighter. "Who are you to judge my life?"

Hiller chuckled. "At least I don't screw up people's lives just in an attempt to get laid."

He lunged toward Hiller, but stopped as a black SUV parked in front of the house.

Detective Lawrence stepped out and looked over at Hiller and then him. "Hey, Jensen. I got something you're going to like."

Unless it was a bat to pummel Hiller with, he was going to be disappointed.

Hiller barked instructions as he walked toward the firefighters. "Hose one needs to be moved around back!" he yelled, pointing toward a west-facing window.

Kevin walked over to Lawrence. "What is it?"

"You and Hiller making nicey-nice again?"

Kevin flipped him off. "What did you find?"

"I just left Truck Boys. I have all of their security footage from the past two weeks. I'm thinking you'll find what you need in it." Lawrence looked over at Heather's house. "You think this one's connected to the others?"

"I haven't had a chance to get in there yet, but based on the fire pattern and Heather's observations, the perp may have used gas. Ran the fire all the way to her bed. Whoever did this wasn't trying to scare her. This time I think they were going for the kill."

"Why do you think they didn't just kill her outright? A gun's a hell of a lot easier than setting a fire."

Kevin nodded. "Whoever set this fire is angry about something and they want to get back at someone, but they aren't the type who wants blood directly on their hands."

"If they kill someone in a fire, their hands aren't clean."

"No, but it's a passive kill. God's will kind of thing."

"You think whoever's behind this could be a woman?"

Kevin thought for a moment. "It could be, but I doubt it. Besides, Heather doesn't have any female enemies."

"No, but based on what you told me about her husband, he might. Maybe it was one of his spurned lovers. Someone who wanted him all to herself?"

"It would make sense, but it doesn't feel right."

Lawrence leaned against his car, crossing his arms over his chest. "You think it's the husband?"

He shook his head. "I think he's in the clear. He's been in surgery for the past three hours. This has to be someone else's work."

"Was Heather sleeping with another man?"

She was sleeping with someone, all right, but he was never going to tell Lawrence.

"She's in the clear."

Heather was talking to Lindsay, but she glanced over at him as if she could tell he was thinking of her and what they had done…and what he wanted to do again.

"What are you thinking?" Lawrence continued.

"I'm thinking Heather's lucky to be alive." He paused. "Whoever's behind this wanted to show their strength. Show they were in control. They want us to fear them—and they wanted to get rid of any possible witnesses by taking Heather out. If we don't get him, I doubt Heather will make it out of this alive."

Lawrence looked toward Heather and a grimace flickered over his normally stoic features. He pulled out a DVD case. "We'll find something."

"We may not. Whoever is behind this is smart. He knows what he's doing."

"But he still made a few mistakes."

"Yeah, but we'll see how far that takes us."

"WHAT'RE YOU GOING to do, Heather?" Lindsay asked, letting go of her waist.

She shrugged. She didn't have a clue. Everything she owned was in that house. Even the G-string she'd found was gone. Now there was no chance of her getting her life in order for the divorce. Add to that the fact that Kevin must think she hated him. And now someone was trying to kill her.

She gave a hysterical laugh.

"You okay?" Colter asked, frowning.

She laughed harder. "I'm fine. Really."

"Then why are you laughing? This can't be funny."

"It's not funny at all. But sometimes when things are this—" She stopped before she said "terrible." Lindsay and Colter didn't need to worry about her. "When things are this *crazy* all you can do is laugh. All I can do is roll with the punches."

Things couldn't get worse.

Lindsay looked at her as though she'd lost her mind and she tried to gain control of her hysterics. This wasn't her. She didn't just lose it. She bit her lip until tears welled in her eyes and there was an iron taste in her mouth.

"You need to take a break. I'll call Brittany," Colter said, taking her by the arm as he led her toward his house.

She sat down on Kevin's couch.

Colter took Lindsay by the hand. "If you need us, Mrs. Samps—Heather—we'll be outside."

She nodded as the door closed quietly behind them. As it clicked, she slumped down, pressing her face into the pillows. All she could smell was tarry smoke. It attacked her senses, its odor reminding her of exactly how powerless she was.

She got up and made her way down the hall to Kevin's room. She grabbed a T-shirt and a pair of shorts that were heaped on the end of his bed. She lifted the clothes to her nose and took in his scent, manly and strong. He smelled so good.

His bed was unmade and wrinkled where their bodies had melded. If only that moment could've lasted, if life had taken a break and let her recover. Instead it had pounded on, wrestling her to the ground.

She sat down on the edge of the bed and ran her fingers over the ridges of his sheets. Kevin could never love the mess that was her and her life. He deserved so much better.

Making her way to the shower, she set his clothes on the sink and turned on the water. The steam rose around her, making the world disappear. She stepped into the water and let it run down her back and over her heated flesh. Her legs were red where the fire had tried to nip at her, but luckily she had no serious burns.

She had been lucky.

She watched as the ashy remnants of her former life swirled down the drain.

There was a knock on the door.

"Yeah? Kevin?" she called, trying to wipe the water from her face.

The door opened.

"Kevin, is that you?" She rubbed her eyes.

She got no answer before the shower curtain was pulled back.

Stephen Hiller stood looking at her with a double-headed ax in his hand.

Heather gasped.

"Get out. Put on a towel," he ordered.

She stepped out of the shower, water dripping from her and pooling on the floor. She pulled a towel from the rack and wrapped it around her. "What're you doing? The fire's not here." As she spoke, fear crept through her.

"I didn't want to do this." Hiller gave her a desperate look. "Why couldn't you just die?"

"I…I…" she stammered. "I don't even know you. What did I do?"

The man snorted. "You wouldn't understand. Your death… It makes sense."

"What're you talking about?"

"Come on now, I've been watching you. Your marriage is a joke. Your husband's a liar, but you buy into it—you're just like him. You are part of the problem, Heather. Don't you realize all those fake smiles and attempts to appease him can come to an end? You don't have to hurt anymore. You can be free of everything. You can make a real difference. You can die for a higher purpose."

"I don't understand," she said, her voice frantic.

"It would help so many people, Heather. You could be a martyr."

She inched toward the door. If she could just get out, maybe she could survive.

"I don't want to be a martyr. I want to live." She inched forward. "You're a fireman. Don't you want to save lives?"

"That's the point. Your death would raise awareness. People would be called to action. Right now, fires happen to *other* people, not them." Hiller twisted the ax in his hands. "Because of this head-in-the-sand attitude, the city and taxpayers don't want to fund us. The people don't understand."

He looked her square in the eyes. All she could see was darkness looking back at her. "You could fix all that. Your death would make people realize arson could happen to them. They would fund our programs and we could really help people instead of getting caught up in bureaucratic games."

"Is that why you chose Brittany and Elke? To send a message?" She slid her foot closer to the door.

He chuckled. "They're nothing but sluts."

She jerked. Brittany wasn't a slut, but she bit her tongue. She wouldn't argue with a potential killer.

"They needed to know fear. They need to always look over their shoulders for what they've done."

"Everyone makes mistakes."

"They were sleeping with your husband. That's one hell of a mistake." He laughed, setting the head of the ax on the floor. "The other day, when you came home and David was on the couch, Elke was upstairs. She was hiding in the guest room."

"How do you know that?"

Hiller gave a large toothy smile; his canines glistened like a carnivore's who was waiting to feast. "I've been watching... Always watching. When Brittany has sex with your husband she likes to be on top."

The man was lying. Brittany wouldn't have slept with David. She was her friend. She had tried to help her win David back.

"You're lying."

"No, I'm not. I thought you'd see Brittany's underwear and figure it all out... Didn't you?"

She looked down at the floor as she thought about the panties she'd retrieved from her sheets. This man had put them there. He had been in her bed. Goose bumps rose on her arms.

"It wasn't just that slut Brittany's fault. No. It all started with that stupid waitress. I gave her so much money, so many tips...but did she even look at me once? No. But in walked your husband and all of a sudden it was like she flipped. She became a teenage girl, giggling and laughing at all his stupid jokes. She couldn't get enough of him. It didn't take long before she took him home."

"So that's why you set the fire at Elke's—you were jealous?"

"I told you," he growled. "She needed to be taught a lesson." He picked the ax up. "Just like the city does."

"Were you in love with Brittany, too?"

"I didn't know her until I started watching David. She was a useful tool to get back at your husband for stealing Elke."

"What about your message to the community?"

"Two birds with one stone, Heather. Two birds." He stared at her. "If things had gone like I planned, no one would've ever known I was involved. No one would've guessed. Then you saw me at Brittany's. Why did you have to look out that window?"

"I didn't see you. I only saw a shadow."

"No, you saw me. Don't lie. It's too late to save yourself."

"If you let me go, I won't tell anyone. I promise. No one has to know you're behind this."

"You know that's a lie. You're friends with Kevin. You could never keep something like this from him. You're just like Allison. That's why he's in love with you."

"He's not…"

"You know he loves you. You have to. Even I can see the way he looks at you. Why do you keep trying to lie to me? I told you. I don't want to kill you, but every time you lie it makes it a little easier."

"There has to be another way. Tie me up. Leave me here. Run. No one will find me for a little while. I'll give you twenty-four hours before I talk to anyone. Even Kevin. I won't say anything. I promise."

Hiller shook his head as he raised the ax. "Let's just get this over with."

She moved fast, unthinking, her fist connecting with his nose with a dull crunch. He stepped back and bumped against the sink as he put his hand to his face. Blood poured from his nose, but he looked up at her with pain and fury in his eyes.

She rushed past him, but as her hand touched the doorknob, his foot connected with the middle of her back like a steel ram and slammed her down to the floor.

"I was wrong, Heather. Killing you is going to be easy."

Chapter Twenty-Four

The video from the tool store was grainy, and if it hadn't been on a DVD Kevin would have been convinced it was a video from the 1980s. He sat in Detective Lawrence's SUV with a laptop on the dash, looking through what felt like a hundred hours of video before he noticed a man walk in the main door that fit the perp's description—dark-haired, stocky, mid to late forties. But his back was to the camera as he walked down the aisle and stopped in front of the brake fluid.

Lawrence tried to zoom in on the man, but there was a glitch and the man in the video went out of focus. "Damn it. Why don't these stores spend a little more money on their security?"

"It's easier and cheaper to let people steal a few bottles of oil than to integrate a new system."

Lawrence huffed. "Ridiculous."

The man in the video turned, keeping his head down, and walked to the counter. It was almost as if the man knew he was being videotaped and was trying to keep from being identified. However, as he moved to hand the cashier some bills, his head rose just enough to glimpse his face.

"Stop. Right there," Kevin said, pointing to the video. "That's our man."

"How do you know?" Lawrence asked with a frown.

"He knows he's being watched. Look at the way he walks." He skipped backward so Lawrence could see the man move.

"You're right. He won't look up."

"But he does…right…here," Kevin said, pausing the video. "Can you pull up a larger image of his face? Anything that would distinguish him?"

Lawrence pressed the buttons on the computer, zooming in on the image and trying to sharpen it as he went. This time, the face came into focus.

"Holy crap," Lawrence whispered. "Can you believe it?"

Before him on the screen, zoomed in so close that he could read the last name on the man's coat, was Stephen Hiller.

He looked out the car window trying to spot the BC, but the man wasn't in the Sampsons' yard. "Where the hell is he?"

Lawrence saved the image and slammed the computer shut. "Isn't he out there?"

Kevin jumped out of the SUV, his eyes searching for one other person. "Heather's gone, too. We need to find her."

"I'll take a look around the house."

Kevin barely heard him.

"Heather!" he called into the mass of firefighters, police officers, neighbors and bystanders who milled around the scene.

There was no answer.

"Heather! Has anyone seen Heather Sampson?"

Colter strode toward him. "It's okay, Dad. She's fine. She just needed a rest. Lindsay and I took her into our house."

He pushed past his son.

"What's going on?" Colter called after him.

"Stay outside with Lindsay."

He rushed across the yard and to his house.

The shower was running in the master suite. "Heather?" he called as he made his way into his bedroom.

Hiller wasn't the kind to kill an innocent woman. Then again, he never thought Hiller was the kind who would be behind a string of arsons.

"Heather?" he called again.

She must not have been able to hear him.

Steam crept out from under the door of his bathroom.

He tapped on the door. "Hey, you in there? Answer me," he yelled.

"Yep… I'm here," she called back, but her voice was hoarse and tight.

"You okay?"

"Fine," she said stiffly.

"Do you need anything?"

There was a long pause and the sound of some muffled movement from behind the door.

She must have been drying off.

He was freaking out over nothing.

"Heather?" he asked, trying to sound calm, but his voice came out strangled and high. "I just found out some things I think you'll want to know. Is it okay if I come in? You decent?"

"No!" she shouted. "Don't come in!"

Something was up. He could feel it. She sounded wrong.

He reached down and twisted the handle. Locked.

"Open the door."

Something inside the bathroom fell to the floor, followed by the sound of a body hitting the wall.

He threw his weight against the door. It cracked, but the lock held. He threw himself against it again.

Her scream pierced the air as something smashed to the floor.

Throwing all his power into it, his body connected with the door one more time, and the frame gave way.

Heather was pinned against a wall, wrapped in a towel, her body pressed against the towel rack. Standing in the middle of the bathroom, blood running down his hand, was Stephen Hiller. The bathroom mirror was broken, its glass sprayed around the floor, and an ax was wedged into the wall where the mirror had once been.

"Hiller... What're you doing?"

The man's eyes were dark and swollen, as though he'd taken a hit to the nose, and there was a smudge of blood where he must have wiped it away.

"I didn't want to take things this far. I never wanted to take things this far," he mumbled. "Now you're going to have to die, too. I didn't want to have to kill anyone." He turned to reach for the ax wedged in the wall.

Kevin lunged toward him. Hiller's fist connected with his cheek, making his head spin. Everything around him slowed as he struggled to remain conscious. Only one thought kept him from slipping into oblivion. Heather needed him.

He swung his fist blindly, glad when it slammed into Hiller's gut.

"You're under arrest," Kevin said, even as he struggled to regain his balance.

But Hiller would not be stopped. He rushed at him. His head connected with Kevin's sternum, sending him to the ground, his breath exhaling in a whoosh. Heather screamed as Hiller moved for the ax.

Hiller grunted as he tried to dislodge the ax. As he struggled, his new boots slipped in the puddle of water on the floor. His feet slipped out from under him. As he fell, his eyes were wide and searching. His head connected with the porcelain toilet with a sickening crunch that reverberated in the bathroom. When his head jerked back, the hatred in his eyes had disappeared, replaced by a lifeless void.

"Heather." Kevin rushed to her and pulled her into his arms. "I should've never let you go. I'm so sorry. I didn't know."

"I'm okay," she said in a voice no louder than an exhale.

He pulled back and he looked her over. The only blood on her seemed to come from her feet, where she must have stepped on the glass from the mirror.

He picked her up, taking her in his arms and carried her out of the house and to the safety of the crowd.

An EMT ran toward them. "Here, I'll take her!" the man offered.

Kevin shook his head. "I'm not letting her go. Not until she's safe."

Lawrence ran around from the back of the house. "Did you find Hiller?"

"He's in my bathroom. He…he's dead."

Epilogue

The snow was falling as Heather made her way across the street. Kevin stood by his truck, waiting with a black bag in his hand. She waved, the cold nibbling at her fingers as she made her way toward him.

"How did it go?" he asked as she stopped beside him.

"Good." She hopped from foot to foot trying to stave off the cold. "But I'm starving," she said, pointing down the street toward the restaurant.

Kevin took her hand, his sudden warmth penetrating the thin cloth of her glove. "What did the judge decide?"

"The divorce is final. All assets are going to be split evenly. David has to pay me alimony for the next five years, long enough for me to go to school." She wrapped her fingers in his, as her excitement filled her. "As for the house, now that everything is fixed, I get it free and clear. I think I may keep it."

"So you're staying there just because it's paid for? No other reason?" Kevin asked with a mischievous grin. "It has nothing to do with who it's next to?"

She returned his grin. "What can I say? Location, location, location."

"I'll take what I can get, but you know you could always move in with me."

She wrapped her other hand over their entwined fingers. "Are you sure you're ready for that? Sure the kids are ready? The therapist said—"

"I know it's fast. If you're not ready—"

"That's not it," she interrupted. "It's just that—"

He stopped walking, the bag in his hand swinging heavily to a stop against his thigh. "I love you, Heather. The kids love you."

Her heart skipped a beat. She had waited for him to say that for so long. "I…I…" she stammered.

"Don't feel like you have to answer now, but…" He got down on one knee and reached into the black bag. He drew out a large, pink box with a black ribbon on top.

"What's that?"

His hands shook slightly, making the box quiver. "Would you please have a piece of cheesecake with me?" he asked with a nervous laugh.

She laughed, cupping her hands over her mouth. "You're crazy. What made you think of that?" She could hardly believe he remembered how much she loved cheesecake.

"Will you?" he repeated, lifting the box higher.

"Absolutely, but you didn't have to get down on your knee for cake."

"Actually, I think I do." He opened up the box.

Inside, on top of the white, creamy cheesecake was a small black velvet box. He set the cake box down on the sidewalk and drew out the smaller box.

"Heather, I know this is fast. You don't have to say yes, but I can't stand it anymore." He opened the box to reveal a diamond solitaire engagement ring. "I love you. I will always love you. I want you in my life. You've been my best friend and helped me through things I never would have made it through if it hadn't been for you. You are the first thing I think of in the morning and the last thing I think of at night. I want you to be my forever. We don't have to do it right away, but… Will you marry me?"

A crowd of people started to form around them on the sidewalk, but she didn't care. She stared at him, at the soft lines around his mouth as he spoke and the glimmer of hope in his eyes. She loved him. She'd loved him almost from the first moment they had met. Her dreams were coming true. It was so surreal.

"Yes… Yes… I love you, too. I will marry you."

He slipped the ring on her finger and stood up. Their warm breath mingled together in the cold, creating a misty cloud around them. She stood on her tiptoes and kissed his lips as he wrapped her in his arms.

He tasted like fresh air, frost and new beginnings.

She leaned back. "I love you so much," she whispered.

His lips took hers, tender and hard in their need, a need that echoed hers.

Life was messy, and things wouldn't be easy, but she was ready. No matter what was to come, they could rise up from the ashes and create a life filled with happiness and possibilities—a world of dreams.

* * * * *

REQUEST YOUR FREE BOOKS!
2 FREE NOVELS PLUS 2 FREE GIFTS!

HARLEQUIN®

INTRIGUE

BREATHTAKING ROMANTIC SUSPENSE

YES! Please send me 2 FREE Harlequin® Intrigue novels and my 2 FREE gifts (gifts are worth about $10). After receiving them, if I don't wish to receive any more books, I can return the shipping statement marked "cancel." If I don't cancel, I will receive 6 brand-new novels every month and be billed just $4.74 per book in the U.S. or $5.49 per book in Canada. That's a savings of at least 12% off the cover price! It's quite a bargain! Shipping and handling is just 50¢ per book in the U.S. and 75¢ per book in Canada.* I understand that accepting the 2 free books and gifts places me under no obligation to buy anything. I can always return a shipment and cancel at any time. Even if I never buy another book, the two free books and gifts are mine to keep forever.

182/382 HDN GH3D

Name   (PLEASE PRINT)

Address   Apt. #

City   State/Prov.   Zip/Postal Code

Signature (if under 18, a parent or guardian must sign)

Mail to the **Reader Service:**
IN U.S.A.: P.O. Box 1867, Buffalo, NY 14240-1867
IN CANADA: P.O. Box 609, Fort Erie, Ontario L2A 5X3

**Are you a subscriber to Harlequin® Intrigue books
and want to receive the larger-print edition?
Call 1-800-873-8635 or visit www.ReaderService.com.**

* Terms and prices subject to change without notice. Prices do not include applicable taxes. Sales tax applicable in N.Y. Canadian residents will be charged applicable taxes. Offer not valid in Quebec. This offer is limited to one order per household. Not valid for current subscribers to Harlequin Intrigue books. All orders subject to credit approval. Credit or debit balances in a customer's account(s) may be offset by any other outstanding balance owed by or to the customer. Please allow 4 to 6 weeks for delivery. Offer available while quantities last.

Your Privacy—The Reader Service is committed to protecting your privacy. Our Privacy Policy is available online at www.ReaderService.com or upon request from the Reader Service.

We make a portion of our mailing list available to reputable third parties that offer products we believe may interest you. If you prefer that we not exchange your name with third parties, or if you wish to clarify or modify your communication preferences, please visit us at www.ReaderService.com/consumerschoice or write to us at Reader Service Preference Service, P.O. Box 9062, Buffalo, NY 14240-9062. Include your complete name and address.

HI15

Her gaze darted up to meet his, and he felt her skin warming
beneath his touch before she turned her hand to squeeze
his fingers. Then she pulled away to finish packing. "But
we've already been too much of an imposition. You need
to go by St. Luke's to visit your grandfather and spend
time with your family. I've already kept you from them
longer than you planned this morning. I can grab the car
seat and call a cab so you don't even have to drive us.
Tommy and I will be fine—as long as you don't mind us
staying in your apartment. Maintenance said there was a
chance they could get someone to see to my locks today."

"And they also said it could be Monday morning." No.
Tommy needed Dr. Niall Watson of the KCPD Crime Lab
to be his friend right now. And no matter how independent
she claimed to be, Lucy needed a friend, too. Right now
that friend was going to be him. Niall shrugged into
his black KCPD jacket and picked up the sweater coat

she'd draped over the back of her chair. "I work quickly and methodically, Lucy. I will find the answers you and Tommy need. But I can't do that when I'm not able to focus. And having half the city between you and me when we don't know what all this means or if you and Tommy are in any kind of danger—"

"Are you saying I'm a distraction?"

Nothing but. Confused about whether that was some type of flirtatious remark or whether she was simply seeking clarification, Niall chose not to answer. Instead, he handed her the sweater and picked up Tommy in his carrier. "Get his things and let's go."

Don't miss APB: BABY
by USA TODAY *bestselling author Julie Miller,*
available June 2016 wherever
Harlequin® Intrigue books and ebooks are sold.

www.Harlequin.com

Reading Has Its Rewards

Earn **FREE BOOKS!**

Register at **Harlequin My Rewards** and submit your Harlequin purchases from wherever you shop to earn points for free books and other exclusive rewards.

Plus submit your purchases from now till May 30th for a chance to win a $500 Visa Card*.

Visit **HarlequinMyRewards.com** today

MYR16R1

THE WORLD IS BETTER WITH

Romance

Harlequin has everything from contemporary, passionate and heartwarming to suspenseful and inspirational stories.

Whatever your mood, we have a romance just for you!

Connect with us to find your next great read, special offers and more.

f /HarlequinBooks

t @HarlequinBooks

www.HarlequinBlog.com

www.Harlequin.com/Newsletters

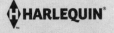

H HARLEQUIN®

A *Romance* FOR EVERY MOOD™

www.Harlequin.com

Love the Harlequin book
you just read?

Your opinion matters.

Review this book on your favorite
book site, review site, blog or your own
social media properties and share
your opinion with other readers!

Be sure to connect with us at:
Harlequin.com/Newsletters
Facebook.com/HarlequinBooks
Twitter.com/HarlequinBooks